HARD TIMES
FOR
JAKE SMITH

Also by Aileen Kilgore Henderson

The Monkey Thief

The Summer of the Bonepile Monster

Treasure of Panther Peak

HARD TIMES for JAKE SMITH

Aileen Kilgore Henderson

MILKWEED  EDITIONS

© 2004, Text by Aileen Kilgore Henderson
All rights reserved. Except for brief quotations in critical articles or reviews, no part of this book may be reproduced in any manner without prior written permission from the publisher: Milkweed Editions, 1011 Washington Avenue South, Suite 300, Minneapolis, Minnesota 55415. (800) 520-6455 / www.milkweed.org / www.worldashome.org

Published 2004 by Milkweed Editions
Printed in Canada
Cover and interior design by Christian Fünfhausen
Cover photographs courtesy of Brown Studio, Minnesota Historical Society (foreground photo) and the Franklin D. Roosevelt Library (background photo).
Author photo by Bob Cleere
The text of this book is set in Goudy Old Style BT Roman.
04 05 06 07 08   5 4 3 2 1
First Edition

Milkweed Editions, a nonprofit publisher, gratefully acknowledges support from Emilie and Henry Buchwald; Bush Foundation; Cargill Foundation; Timothy and Tara Clark Family Charitable Fund; DeL Corazón Family Fund; Dougherty Family Foundation; Ecolab Foundation; Joe B. Foster Family Foundation; General Mills Foundation; Jerome Foundation; Kathleen Jones; Constance B. Kunin; D. K. Light; Chris and Ann Malecek; McKnight Foundation; a grant provided by the Minnesota State Arts Board, through an appropriation by the Minnesota State Legislature, a grant from the Wells Fargo Foundation Minnesota, and a grant from the National Endowment for the Arts; Sheila C. Morgan; Laura Jane Musser Fund; National Endowment for the Arts; Navarre Corporation; Kate and Stuart Nielsen; Outagamie Charitable Foundation; Qwest Foundation; Debbie Reynolds; St. Paul Companies, Inc., Foundation; Ellen and Sheldon Sturgis; Surdna Foundation; Target, Marshall Field's, and Mervyn's with support from the Target Foundation; Gertrude Sexton Thompson Charitable Trust; James R. Thorpe Foundation; Toro Foundation; Weyerhaeuser Family Foundation; and Xcel Energy Foundation.

Library of Congress Cataloging-in-Publication Data

Henderson, Aileen Kilgore, 1921–
    Hard times for Jake Smith / Aileen Kilgore Henderson. — 1st ed.
      p. cm.
    Summary: In 1935 Alabama, when twelve-year-old MaryJake is abandoned by her financially strapped parents and told to walk to the house of unknown relatives, she dresses like a boy and joins the household of an old widow before discovering secrets about her own family.
    ISBN 1-57131-649-3 (pbk. : alk. paper) — ISBN 1-57131-648-5 (hardcover : alk. paper)
    [1. Family—Fiction. 2. Identity—Fiction. 3. Abandoned children—Fiction. 4. Depressions—History—Fiction. 5. Disguise—Fiction. 6. Alabama—History—20th century—Fiction.] I. Title.
PZ7.H37874Har 2004
[Fic]—dc22

2003020508

To my sisters:

Francys Ruth, Annie Jane, and Mary Alice

HARD TIMES
⫯⫯ FOR ⫯⫯
JAKE SMITH

ONE

MARYJAKE KNEW SOMETHING was getting ready to happen, something that she was being kept in the dark about, something her parents were plotting between them. She knew whatever it was they intended to do would affect her life in a way she didn't like. Else why were they shutting her out?

Maybe they were planning to move again, but always before MaryJake had been a part of the "relocating," as her father called it. They had relocated many times, twice in the last six months. As far back as she could remember, she had helped load the wagon and taken care of her two little brothers. The last move, after her twelfth birthday in this year of 1935, she held the reins and guided the mule by herself. Her father had tramped behind the wagon with his twenty-two rifle, searching the bushes for a rabbit to put in the supper pot. MaryJake's being involved in the changes had made them seem less like an uprooting and more like a usual occurrence. She never grieved, even though each move brought the family to a more dilapidated house where they had less food to eat and fewer chairs to sit on.

But now her mother and father spoke words to each other that did not make sense to MaryJake. Incidents took place that she could not understand. The "disappearances" were the most worrisome. Sometimes she could think of a reasonable explanation, and her worry would lie quiet for a while. For instance, their crippled mule had died during the winter, so it was sensible her father would sell the harness and plow stock, because they had no money to buy another mule.

But the disappearance of Katura, the old sow who looked like a bag of oats with ears, couldn't be explained as easily. Twice a year Katura birthed a dozen piglets of assorted designs—solid black, solid peach, spotted, and striped. MaryJake slopped the pigs, dug Johnson grass roots for them to eat, and drew up water from the depths of the well to fill their bathing pool. She and her brothers played with each set of piglets, trained them to "talk," sit on their hind legs, and play hide-and-seek, keeping in mind that eventually Pa would sell them or turn them into meat for the table. Katura was valuable—a moneymaker and a food producer. How could she vanish?

One Saturday her father led Rose, their milk cow, down the road and out of sight without a word to MaryJake, who had named her Cherokee Rose and raised her from an orphan calf. MaryJake took full-time care of her. She kept Rose's drinking tub filled with fresh well water. She roamed far fields, accompanied by her dog, Adder, to cut armloads of tender grass for Rose night and morning. MaryJake curried Rose's Jersey coat, the color of rich cream, till it shone.

Whenever the cow tangled with barbed wire, MaryJake made a slippery elm poultice to keep the ragged cuts from becoming infected. In contrary moments, MaryJake felt like Rose's servant, but most of the time she didn't mind because Rose was such a beautiful, calm, trusting cow. She gave good milk and cream to keep the two little brothers plump, and buttermilk to eat with cornbread for supper every night. What were they going to do without Rose?

But the worst day was when MaryJake came home from school and went, as was her habit, to collect eggs from the nests in the shed. The nests were empty. No busy hens ran about the yard scratching up worms and bugs, and no proud rooster bossed them. An eerie feeling chilled her, standing there in the silent yard with Adder leaning against the leg of her overalls. The vanishing of the industrious chickens, which made no trouble, found their own food, and produced eggs and meat for the family, frightened her more than the other disappearances. What—or who—would be next? Would she discover one day that her brothers had disappeared? Or Adder? She squatted down to put her arms around her dog, to hold him close. He wouldn't vanish, she was sure, because he was completely hers and nobody else's. But the scary feeling that her parents had turned into strangers wouldn't leave her.

Often lately MaryJake forgot the unbreakable family rule: Young'uns don't ask questions. The first time or two she forgot, her parents played deaf. But when she persisted, her father lost patience and lashed out. "Hold your tongue, MaryJake. You'll know soon enough."

It seemed to MaryJake that her father's anger was not *at* her, but she knew it was *about* her. Had she done anything wrong? She tried harder than ever to move about the house without clomping, to draw enough water out of the well to keep the buckets filled, to wash her brothers clean and keep them quiet. She chopped wood for the cookstove and carried armloads of it to the kitchen to keep the wood box filled. She didn't talk back. Her struggle to keep her mouth shut made her jaws ache. She was obedient.

Nobody noticed, and whatever was afoot continued to grow undercover like a live thing and to move ahead to certain calamity. MaryJake had steeled herself against it, but when it sprang on a breezy April morning, she was unprepared.

After breakfast Pa said to her, "Don't feed the dog this morning."

MaryJake, who was already collecting bits of bread and gravy from the little boys' plates for Adder, stopped short. "Don't feed Adder?"

"You heard me the first time. Don't give the dog food. Or water."

"How come?" Like a dying fish she had to keep her mouth open to gasp for breath.

Pa shoved his chair away from the table. "He's got to take a ride in the car. I don't want him puking on the seats." He strode toward the bedroom, clearing his throat and making a lot of noise with his heavy shoes.

MaryJake forgot obedience. She could think only of Adder. She raced after Pa, her bare feet thumping the wood floor. "What—Why—How come?" she demanded, grabbing his arm and hanging on with her whole weight as he tried to keep moving away. He shook her off, jabbing her in the side with his sharp elbow so that she fell back against the wall.

"Shet the dog in the corncrib," he ordered. "Now!" He turned his ferocious eyes full on her. It was as if he had struck her again. "Or else!" Her stunned mind heard an echo: Or else you'll be next.

She backed away, and he slammed the bedroom door. Her chest tightened into a knot that racked her whole body with the pain of it. Through a dark haze she saw Paul and David sitting on upturned boxes at the table, silent and big eyed. Her mother faced the window, washing dishes. MaryJake knew they could give her no help.

What was he going to do with Adder? Shoot him? Take him away and abandon him on some road far from home? She crept out on the porch. Adder was waiting in the yard. He came trotting toward her, eyes expectant, swallowing to keep his saliva under control. Without a word or a pat, she took him to the corncrib and pushed him in, shutting her eyes against his puzzled expression. But she couldn't shut her ears against the unspoken words that had hung between her father and her in the kitchen: *Or else you'll be next.*

TWO

MARYJAKE HID under the high porch below the great green elephant-eared plants with stalks as big as her arms. She crouched, not like a girl with a head and two arms and two legs, but like a lump. Cool sunlight strained through the gold-green leaves. The quiet closed in around her. The only turmoil was inside her, trying to burst out.

The floorboards overhead creaked as Ma came to the porch to throw away the dishwater. The water spattered like rain on the giant leaves spread under the edge of the porch. Droplets rolled about on the upper sides of the leaves like silver clouds casting transparent shadows in a green sky. The porch shook with Ma's quick steps. The screen door slapped to as she returned inside. Quiet again. MaryJake pressed her hands to her throbbing neck and tried to soothe her burning face. She sat still and tight.

The kitchen door opened and slammed shut. MaryJake watched a glob of water tremble on a leaf as heavy feet walked to the top of the high steps. Pa. Then the door opened and shut softly; quick footsteps followed the heavy ones. Ma.

"Isn't there any way she can keep him?" she said. Ma would be twisting her hands in her apron. "She's always thought so much of him—"

"No way a'tall." He clipped the words out before she finished speaking. "Time she larned you can't keer too much fer a dog. Or anything else, fer that matter."

"I hate to see her left with nothing—with nobody." They were both still, standing at the top of the steps above MaryJake's head.

"No other way," he said. "We got to have the money. Folks pay a lot for a fightin' dog. More'n enough to get us halfway there."

He came down the steps, placing his feet in the exact middle. MaryJake watched each plank bend in turn under his weight. She shifted her position to watch Pa walk in his double-jointed way to the corncrib and come out pulling Adder by a rope around his neck. Her eyes focused on Adder, bracing his stout legs and his white powerful body against the pull, his pinkish eyes sharp on Pa, his pointed ears and pointed nose trying to figure out what was going on before agreeing to it.

"Come along here now," Pa ordered, dragging Adder across the bare swept yard toward the topless Model T Ford he had bought secondhand. MaryJake remembered that the appearance of the car was the first of all the strange happenings. Adder looked back over his shoulder. MaryJake knew he was looking for her. He couldn't understand why he was going somewhere without her, somewhere that required the car for transportation instead of his strong white feet.

Though she tried to watch him go, tears blinded her. She hugged her legs, rocking back and forth, pressing her face hard against her bony kneecaps and crying silently. The worn cloth of her overalls absorbed the tears like a blotter, holding them warm and wet against her skin. Adder had been her dog for every day of the four years since she found him standing by the road, looking toward the curve where the road went out of sight. MaryJake didn't know how long he had been waiting when she came along, walking home from school. She was eight years old—that was seven moves ago—and not too nervy, but as soon as she saw him she knew he was meant for her. He made it clear that he didn't feel the same way. He looked at MaryJake when she talked to him, but she could tell his mind was somewhere else. His gaze went over her shoulder to the distant curve of the road, expecting his folks to come back for him any minute, she guessed.

After a while, MaryJake continued her walk home thinking about how his ribs showed, how scarred his white-fur bodysuit was, and how ragged his ears. The mule and wagon were gone from the yard; that meant Pa wasn't home. Ma was picking peas, stooped over in the garden a little distance from the house. MaryJake's two brothers, scarcely out of babyhood, lay limp in sleep on a quilt spread over the porch floor.

Her bare feet had made no sound as she went into the open hall, laid her books on a straight chair, and headed for the kitchen. She found what she expected—a plate of cornbread covered with a clean towel and on the stove an iron pot of greens cooked with fatback. She split open a piece of cornbread, layered it with pork fat to make a sandwich, and slipped it in the pocket of her overalls. Next problem, water. What could she carry water in that would also be all right for the dog to drink from? She found a berry-picking bucket, stained dark red from last year's berries, and poured it half full of water.

She went about these preparations as quietly as she could. If her brothers awoke, she would have to take care of them. Then she couldn't go back to the dog, and she was determined he wouldn't spend a hungry night by the side of the road.

When she hurried back to him, the dog gulped down the cornbread sandwich almost before she laid it on the ground, and he drank every drop of water. And though she talked to him, and he politely listened, she could tell his mind was on his folks returning for him, and that he needed to finish with her in a hurry so he'd be ready when they arrived.

The dog refused to come home with her until the third day. By then he'd given up hope, she figured. MaryJake hadn't mentioned him to anybody. When she led him into the yard she was nervous about what Pa would say. But he surprised her.

"Well, I'll be," Pa said grinning. "He's one o'them fightin' dogs—worth a pot full o'money. Who'd throw *him* away?"

"Probably somebody with good sense who feared having him around children," Ma said, frowning. Three years of almost perfect dog behavior passed before Ma relaxed and trusted him.

Adder went everywhere with MaryJake and helped her with the chores. At the close of day he could locate Rose wherever she had wandered while grazing in the woods and help MaryJake bring her home for milking. He kept the rabbits and the deer run out of the pea patch. In the potato garden, after MaryJake loosened the soil, Adder burrowed the potatoes out of the dirt with his nose, even the smallest ones, the way a puffing adder snake plowed the ground with its hard nose, getting at grubs and hop-toads. He even puffed and blew his lips like an adder while he was doing it. It was his way of harvesting potatoes that made MaryJake decide on his name.

No stranger could come near the house without Adder notifying everybody. He had moved with them seven times, sitting in MaryJake's lap if there was no space for him, or trotting with her behind the wagon if MaryJake had to walk.

From what she heard said above her on the porch, MaryJake believed Pa would sell Adder for a fighting dog. At school the kids talked about men who gathered in the woods on Sunday afternoons to bet on such fights. They half starved the dogs to make them savage. When two dogs fought, the fight didn't end until one of them lay dead. Sometimes, the men put several dogs together in the fighting pit, watching as they tore each other to shreds.

Something else Pa said—the money from the sale of Adder would be "more than enough to get us halfway there." So we *are* leaving, MaryJake thought, drying her tears on her shirttail. We must be going a long way this time. What had Ma meant when she said, "I hate to see her get left with nothing, with nobody"? MaryJake wouldn't let herself think about that, but she had to accept the fact that Pa had sold Rose and the others. She'd never see any of them again.

A movement caught by the corner of her eye told her she wasn't alone under the house. A little snake, round as a pencil and slick and firm, flowed over the ground through this private green world as if it belonged to him. Jewel-like and deliberate, he propelled himself along like an unhooked bracelet, through the muted sun and shade. His body seemed to taste each grain of the cool earth as he poured himself slowly into the small hollows and flowed as slowly out again. He showed no fear of MaryJake, and she felt no fear of him. He was neither friendly nor unfriendly but moved with confident neutrality. His body was ringed with bands of various widths—wide red, narrow yellow, medium-wide black, narrow yellow, and wide red again. On either side of his black snout, eyes like enameled beads looked secretly at MaryJake as he passed, his tongue darting this way and that, testing the air. MaryJake could have touched him if she had reached out her hand, but she knew he was not harmless like the puffing adder. Without a sound, he slipped into the dimness behind her. Watching him quieted MaryJake's heart. What was trying to burst her chest slowly shrank, like a balloon stretched to its thinnest skin that is relieved when air oozes out of a tiny leak.

THREE

FIVE-YEAR-OLD DAVID came into MaryJake's view. He was searching for her, she knew. In one hand he carried a spray from a sweet shrub bush. He looked right and left as he moved along, and then he stopped square in front of the elephant ears and squatted down, staring under the porch. MaryJake didn't know David suspected her hiding place. She stayed still, but when his eyes adjusted, David saw her without surprise.

"Come out, Sister," he said. "Come out, MayJay." His face tuned up to cry. Suddenly, he laughed, swiping his wet cheeks with a dirty hand. "MayJay, you look like a big green lizard thinkin' 'bout eatin' me."

MaryJake unfolded herself like a rusty jackknife and crawled through the elephant ears out into the sunlight. Still on her knees, she put her arms tightly around David. "I *am* a big green lizard," she growled, "and I will eat you up." She mouthed over his neck and plump arms while he giggled and kicked.

"Where's Paul?" she asked, setting him free.

He pointed toward the field back of the corncrib. "Pickin' flowers. For you, 'cause Adder's gone." He handed her the wilted sweet shrubs that smelled like crushed strawberries.

She took a deep breath. "Ummm, sweet. Now bring Paul." Her bare feet made no sound going up the steps and across the porch. She paused at the door. Through the screen she saw her mother at the table shaking bills and silver money out of the Prince Albert tobacco can. She sorted the bills and stacked the change, counting. The last time MaryJake saw the can it was empty. Now it was fuller than she had ever seen it—money from selling the plowing tools, from selling Katura, Rose, the chickens. When Pa returned, the money for Adder would be added to the can.

She backed away from the door, unable to go in, but her mother called, "MaryJake, I want to talk to you." Ma made the bills into a neat wad, which she crammed back in the narrow can. She raked the change off the table into her hand, dropped it in with the bills, and snapped the cover shut.

She looked at MaryJake. She seldom looked directly at anybody; she looked off to one side of you, as if afraid of seeing things about you that she didn't want to know. But now her eyes, clear green flecked with brown that sometimes turned to gold, nailed MaryJake in place. "You've got to remember there're certain tasks in life a person has to do. Hard tasks. There's no other way, just no other way."

Does she mean Pa and Adder? Or does she mean me and something I have to do? MaryJake wondered, clinging to the table edge to keep herself steady. She broke the rule again. She couldn't help herself. "Where're we going? When?"

The lids dropped over her mother's eyes. She turned the can around in her hand so that Prince Albert in his frock coat faced MaryJake. For a moment MaryJake thought Ma was reading the fine print, that she had forgotten the question. Then Ma whispered, "I don't know." She spoke louder as she stood up and began doing everything at once. "We'll see. And all will be for the best. Remember that."

Ma shoved Pa's chair under the table—it was the only one left and its rungs were broken. She hid the tobacco can behind the cupboard door and ordered, "Make sure your dress and bloomers are clean. Your overalls are past wearing, so is your shirt. Leave them behind. Anyway, you're too old now to be wearing overalls." She pulled out a drawer under the Prince Albert cupboard. MaryJake knew it was empty, but to her surprise Ma took a square fold of cloth out of it. "You'll need a change of clothes. And you must look nice. I've remade one of my old dresses to fit you."

MaryJake's arms, bent at the elbow, held the folded dress out in front of her like a shelf. The cloth was a cool shade of green with white leaves scattered over it. She chose this one to please me, MaryJake thought. She knows how much I love trees and plants. But MaryJake wanted to shout, "Keep your dress! I don't want it!" Holding it in her arms struck her with terror. This was part of their plan. Maybe refusing to accept the dress would bring the plan to a halt.

Paul and David shuffled through the screen door carrying flowers stuck in an old bottle. Her mother closed the drawer, frowning at MaryJake. "Put the dress away for now. Then take your brothers down to the well and give them a good scrubbing and hair washing. Use lots of soap, now, but don't get it in their eyes."

In the bedroom, two mattresses stuffed with corn shucks lay on the floor. Ma and Pa slept on one; David, Paul, and MaryJake slept on the other. Sleeping with the boys wasn't easy. They both kicked in their sleep and gnashed their teeth. Sometimes it seemed to MaryJake she spent most of her time in bed hanging over the floor.

She laid the new dress on top of her neatly folded old dress on the wall shelf. She set the bottle of wildflowers on the floor beside her place on the mattress. Touching each blossom she named them to herself—may apple, sweet shrub, windflower, thimbleweed, meadow rue, bugbane, bouncing bet, Adam-and-Eve, rose pogonia, hoary puccoon, bluebells. Some flower names were as pretty as their blossoms. Others were funny. Her brothers liked to hear MaryJake name them over. Sometimes she showed them pictures of the flowers in a book one of her teachers gave her. The book was the first thing she put in her stack of possessions to take with her.

She thought about Miss Blackwell, at the Three Notch school, who had eaten sweet potatoes every day for lunch till she saved enough money to buy *Wildflowers of Alabama's Forests* for the school's library shelf. MaryJake and the teacher took the book on weekends to hunt wildflowers. They were planning a wild garden for the Three Notch school yard when MaryJake's pa decided to relocate.

Miss Blackwell had said, "MaryJake, this book is yours.

Nobody here will ever crack it open except me, and I'm getting too old to hunt wildflowers. Besides," a sad smile softened her plain face, "I can't go in the woods without you. I'd get lost." MaryJake let herself be convinced because she wanted the book so much for her own.

She thought of these things, standing there in the sleeping room with her hand resting on her stack of possessions. Thinking about the past and worrying about the future would not change what was happening now. She realized there was nothing she could do but wait.

At suppertime a visitor arrived in the front yard. As soon as MaryJake heard the snappy ringing of a bell, she knew it was Miss Celestine and her horse, Dink. Here was a chance to escape from the table, where every bite of beans and bread choked her. She led her brothers in a rush to the front porch.

Pa followed them saying under his breath, "That ole preacher woman! Why would she show up here tonight? Blast—"

Ma brought up the rear, smoothing her hair and straightening her dress. "Of all things!" she muttered. "Her!"

A small black-haired woman was sliding off a red horse taller than her head. A faded bonnet swung from its strings tied around her neck. Her long dark dress swished as she came toward the porch.

"Greetings, friends," she called in a voice that sounded as clear and lively as the bell she had rung to announce her arrival. "I'm passing this way and wondered if I could take shelter with you for the night?" She had reached the edge of the porch but hesitated to raise her small foot to step up on it, squinting her eyes to see who was bunched there in the shadows. "Why, why—it's the Wildsmiths! I never expected to find people I know!" She tossed back her head and laughed, letting it rush up from her middle. "But that's just like God to gift me with old friends right when I'm the neediest." She bent her head in a quick movement and said briskly, "Thank you, Lord!" then stood silent, waiting for a response from the porch.

Pa said, "Hidy do, Miss Celestine. I'm afeerd you caught us short. We can't offer you a bed tonight like we did that time over at Three Notch. And before that at Hurricane Crossroads and before that—." MaryJake knew Pa was making a point naming all the times they had taken in Miss Celestine.

Miss Celestine laughed again. "How well I remember! And my gratitude lives on. But I'm not asking for a bed. If I can spread my pallet here on your porch, and if ole Dink can have a drink of water and a roll in the dust! We've both had a hard hot day, I tell you. Started out at five o'clock this morning over in the next county. But I've got some goodies in my baggage. As soon as I'm settled we'll all have a goody feast."

The two little boys held on to MaryJake's overalls and watched in astonishment. MaryJake doubted if they could remember other visits the family had had from this wandering woman but MaryJake remembered. Her mouth watered as she thought about past goodies Miss Celestine had taken from the flour sacks that hung across Dink's bony back—maybe tea cakes Miss Celestine had made herself, or a sorghum syrup pie from the house where she'd spent the night before. There was bound to be something delicious.

With slow steps, Pa went out to unload the horse.

MaryJake didn't see how Miss Celestine could have ever reached up and lifted off the bundles and bags by herself, she was built so little. Ma directed MaryJake to fetch the broom and sweep off the porch for the pallet while she tidied the supper table. MaryJake heard Dink do a little dance step, blow his lips, and groan as he sank down in the sand spread over the front yard. He stretched out his loosely-put-together body and rolled this way and that.

"Dink is the best roller," Miss Celestine said coming up on the porch with an armload of quilts and sacks. "I used to fear he'd break nature's law and roll all the way over—that'd never do. Bring on a death for sure. An untimely death." Her voice lost not a bit of its brightness as she spoke of this dismal possibility, MaryJake noticed as she helped to spread the two quilts. "Come and see, Miz Wildsmith. Do you know these patterns? When I stayed with Miz Stillwagon—older than Methuselah, she is—across the county line, the two of us pieced these tops and did the quilting while Dink was having a sick spell. This one, the prettiest I think, is 'Barbrie Allen's Rose.' The other one's called 'Castle Dungeon.'" Ma leaned over to get a better look in the dusk, and brushed her fingertips over the quilts as if that would help her see clearer. She studied the stitches, which MaryJake could see were tiny and even.

"They're patterns not known to me," Ma said. "They're very pretty."

Miss Celestine watched Pa watering Dink at the well. "Not too much right at first, Mr. Wildsmith," she called. "Sometimes Dink overdoes the drinking—that's how come he got sick at Miz Stillwagon's. Horses are short on walking-around sense, not like a mule. But good came out of it—the Lord healed Dink and I've got these quilts to show for my time there."

FOUR

MISS CELESTINE'S GOOD CHEER and lively talk gradually relaxed Ma and Pa into a more welcoming frame of mind. Part of their reluctance to take her in, MaryJake knew, was because of what Miss Celestine was—a woman evangelist. They didn't believe a woman should be a preacher. "It ain't biblical," Pa had said. But every time Miss Celestine came wandering into their yard, Ma became entranced all over again with her. Especially with Miss Celestine's account of how the Lord sent her on her mission. She would tell it again tonight, MaryJake was sure. For once she looked forward to hearing the story, hoping it would make her forget for a little while what was happening in her own life.

Another comfortable thing about Miss Celestine—she paid no mind to how they had come down in the world. She never asked questions or looked around with prying eyes. Nobody had the worry of thinking up answers ahead of time for Miss Celestine.

After Dink was watered and staked in a grassy spot for

grazing, the pallet spread, and the bundles stacked against the porch wall, everybody gathered at the kitchen table. Miss Celestine was seated in Pa's chair with the little boys perched atop their boxes on either side of her. Ma and Pa stood together, MaryJake a little apart. The faint light from the lamp—the kerosene was low and they had none to add to it—made Paul's and David's intent eyes appear to be out on stems as they watched Miss Celestine untie and unwrap.

Bananas! MaryJake put her hand over her mouth to stifle a gasp. She had eaten a whole banana once, so long ago she didn't remember who gave it to her. The creamy, boneless taste of it had stayed with her even after she gnawed the bitter inside of the peel.

Miss Celestine used the long blade of her pocketknife to slice two of the bananas crosswise into six even pieces. She handed them around still in their black-freckled yellow skins. David and Paul, once they understood about removing the peel, pushed the whole piece in their mouths at one time. MaryJake ate hers nibble by nibble while Miss Celestine opened a box of pound cake, so golden it had to have been made with butter and at least six eggs. The fine texture trimmed with brown crust made MaryJake's favorite cake a perfection. She sighed, not understanding how she could have such pleasure at the end of a day that broke her heart. They finished what Miss Celestine called their "goody feast" with one store-bought gingersnap each.

Miss Celestine reboxed the pound cake, retied the two remaining bananas, and folded the leftover paper. Pa blew out the lamp. They made their way to the porch in the dark, each one finding a place to settle down on the end away from the pallet. MaryJake dangled her legs off the edge, leaning against a post, with David in her lap and Paul relaxed against her. They were ready.

Miss Celestine wove a spell when she talked, speaking the parts of everyone she told about. "You may not remember," she said out of the darkness, "but it's been three years since the Lord gave me my revelation. Three years since he called me to get on ole Dink and go. It's never easy to discern the Lord's will. At least not for me. But what a joy in the seeking! Even in those first days back where I used to live, when He made me know He had anointed me for a purpose, I couldn't get ahold of His meaning. Twelve Sundays in a row at daybreak, come rain, come shine, He led me to a chestnut log, so old it looked like Jonah's great white whale beached in the woods. I didn't see Him, but He was there, His Holy Presence surrounding me on all sides. Sheltering me from the rain. Shielding me from the lightning. On my knees in the mud at that ole log. Loud I prayed, soft I prayed. Demanding I prayed, pleading I prayed. But all He said was, 'Wait, Celestine. You're not ready to hear me yet.' Think of it! The Lord Himself dealing with me, a nobody, an ole maid girl down on her knees in the mud at a dead-and-gone chestnut tree." She paused to marvel.

The full moon had risen. From the dark porch MaryJake looked out into a world drenched in white light. The only sound was Dink cropping grass. The little boys lay still against her, but they were awake and listening.

"On that twelfth Sunday morning, sharp at sunrise, the revelation came. Right away I could see the sense of the Lord testing me and trying me all those weeks. Else I think I would have turned tail and run when He told me my assignment.

"'Celestine,' he said in a calming voice. 'You are to build a chapel for Me.' As He spoke, in the mist of the forest, I saw a little church with a steeple where a silver bell swung. 'And, Celestine, around My chapel you are to build cottages, cottages for boys without homes, boys nobody wants. Gather them from the highways and the byways, the hedges and the hollows. Don't turn a single one away.'

"I jumped to my feet, looking at the vision of those cottages circled round the chapel. But I wasn't thinking about how pretty they were. 'What a hard thing you are laying on me, Lord. I don't know pea turkey about boys. Why not girls? At least I know a mite about girls, being one myself.'

"'Boys,' the Lord said. 'I have chosen others to rescue the homeless girls.'

"'All that costs money, Lord, Sir. I've got five dollars and sixty cents to my name and owe a bill at the store.'

"'You are mouthing at me, Celestine.'

"'Forgive me, Lord, but I can't understand—build on what land? With whose money? Lord, Lord, I can't do it! It's impossible, what you require of me,' and I broke down crying fit to kill.

"What love was in His voice when He said, 'I am your strength and your help. I am with you always. How can anything be impossible for you?'

"I had no answer to that except, 'I know, Lord. What must I do?'

"And He said, 'Where I want you to build my boys' home is not here. I will show you the place.'

"I was weeping again—I couldn't help myself. 'But, Lord, how can I find it?'

"'Celestine, my daughter, just get on ole Dink and go.'

"And that's what I've done for lo, these three years. Dink and me have searched the highways and the byways, the hedges and the hollows. I've found some likely places, some rich places, places with saintly people willing to do for the Lord, but He's not put his approval on any of them. And so we keep going, ole Dink and me, and the Lord has surely cared for us through the hard times and the easy times. Praise His name!" Everyone sat in silence until Pa cleared his throat and shuffled his shoes.

Then Miss Celestine said, "I thank you for giving me a chance to expand. Every time I tell the story my faith gets bolstered up." She said a short night prayer and wished everybody good sleeping.

In bed MaryJake thought about the Lord and Miss Celestine. She wished she could converse with Him that way. MaryJake talked plenty inside of herself, but she never heard any answers. She needed to know the why and wherefore of so many things. She decided that for now she would ask God to take care of Adder and her, for she had a feeling that they were the ones most in need.

FIVE

MARYJAKE AWOKE TO DARKNESS and the moist waiting feel that early morning air has. Breakfast-making noises came from the kitchen, but it was not nearly time for breakfast. Out in the yard she heard dragging sounds and thumps. Pa, doing something with the car. She hid under the thin quilt, cold and stiff, knowing it was here, it had come, now. Neither God nor Miss Celestine had staved it off.

Ma came softly into the room, bringing fried grease odors with her. In the dark she shook MaryJake by the shoulder. "Get up." She kept her voice low. Paul turned over, rustling the corn shucks, and gave a deep sigh. "Put on your new dress. Tie up your other things in this dish towel. Remember, leave your overalls here. See if you can get your shoes on somehow. Then wake the boys. They can wear their everyday clothes."

We're going, MaryJake thought. But I'm dressing up, and they're not. Why?

She clenched her teeth, but that did not stop her

trembling. Her few things were ready for tying in the bundle. She rolled her overalls and the flimsy shirt as small as her tremulous hands could make them and put them in the bundle too. The soft old clothes took up so little room, Ma would never suspect. The new dress slipped smoothly over her head and hung loose without a belt line. She could see the whiteness of the leaves in the dark. She had just about outgrown her bloomers. The tight elastic squeezed her waist and each of her legs, cutting off the circulation, she was sure.

She felt around in the dark corner for her shoes and shook out the spiders before forcing her feet into them. Then she woke David and Paul, half dragging them through the kitchen to the wash pan on the porch shelf. She saw no trace of Miss Celestine or Dink as she washed the boys' sleep-crusted eyes. With the half comb that stayed on the shelf, she made their hair neat, then her own. Ma barbered the three of them the same way, hair short above their ears all the way round, which made neatness a simple matter. "My three towheads," Ma would say, admiring her work. Without a mirror to linger over, they were soon ready for breakfast.

After a quick, silent meal—Miss Celestine had left her last two bananas to go with the chitterling fritters and biscuits—MaryJake cleaned the few utensils they had used and Ma packed them in a box, which Pa took out to the car. She brought her bundle from the back room and helped the boys with theirs while Ma set the chair straight under the table and stacked the two wood crates—she always left their houses neat. Last thing, she took the Prince Albert can out of the cupboard.

They filed out to the car where Pa waited. He arranged the boys on top of what was packed in the backseat. They looked comfortable, half lying in a nest, surrounded on all sides by boxes. They watched in the morning twilight as Ma sat in the middle of the front seat and told MaryJake to get in beside her. MaryJake fitted her shoe-clad feet in among clay jugs of water—for drinking and the car radiator—and settled her bundle on her lap. Through the thin dish towel she felt the metal fasteners on her overall galluses. Pa came from checking through the house once more and got in under the steering wheel.

With sunrise drawing near, the sky seemed to catch fire and reflect the flames onto the earth. "It's the dust," Ma said, looking up. "Seems as if all of Oklahoma must be blowing over here to Alabama."

"More'n just Oklahoma," Pa said, grinding the car starter. "Texas too."

Grrrrr, grrrrr, the car motor said. Nothing happened. After several more tries, Pa found the crank under the seat, went to the front of the car and bent over to hand crank it. Ma sat under the steering wheel, pushing levers when he shouted directions. MaryJake clutched her bundle, looked straight ahead, and said nothing. The car wouldn't start, but she didn't rejoice. She had the desolate feeling that whether or not the car started, or suddenly jerked into motion and ran over Pa, or the crank reversed and broke his arm, nothing could interfere with what was happening. David and Paul kept still and quiet.

The engine came to life with a cough and a backfire, and Pa drove them out of the yard. East was at their back, but MaryJake knew by the light flooding the world that the sun had come above the treetops. The car took them past MaryJake's school—closed and silent this early—through town, and along a paved road she hadn't seen before. After what seemed like two hours, they came to a wide bare place where a dirt road connected to the one they traveled. Pa pulled to the side and stopped.

"Here's where you get out, MaryJake," he said. "See how this road goes into the woods? You follow that."

Ma said, "Listen carefully, MaryJake. Follow only the road that bears to the left. Do not take the fork to the right. You hear me? The left fork is for you. In a little bit you'll come to a settlement called Rock Castle. The houses, the post office, and the store are clustered around a stone house with turrets—the rock castle, they call it—."

"Don't stop at any house 'cept the rock castle," Pa interrupted, reaching across Ma and gripping MaryJake's arm hard. "No matter who you meet or what they say, go to the rock house."

"Just tell them your name—MaryJake Wildsmith. Give them this." Ma slipped a white handkerchief with a lump in one lacy corner into MaryJake's hand, forcing her numb fingers to close over it. Ma opened the car door. "Do as I say now, the left-hand fork and straight to the rock house, no other." MaryJake could not make herself move.

"She won't do it," Pa said in disgust. "We better carry her there."

"Oh no!" Ma shrank down in the seat. Her voice sounded panicky. "MaryJake will do it. She is an obedient child." And Ma nudged her out of the car.

MaryJake stood by the road, clutching the handkerchief and her bundle, watching the car going west. Two towheads with bowl haircuts raised up out of their nest, looking back at her as long as the car was in sight. She made no movement for a long time, staring at where the car disappeared. She was like Adder the day she found him, but she did not have Adder's hope. She knew her folks were never coming back for her.

SIX

W HEN SHE FINALLY REALIZED she was not going to die in her tracks, she turned toward the dirt road that forked like a slingshot handle. Both forks appeared to be well traveled. MaryJake stared along the right-hand road. What did it lead to? Just to spite Ma and Pa she ought to go that way. She looked at the left-hand road and set her jaw. I'll never go there, rock castle or no rock castle, she thought. Who would the people be in that rock castle? Not kinfolks—Wildsmiths only had kin people near Okolona, Mississippi. Pa had once mentioned his brother who lived there, a man too sorry to eat pie.

As MaryJake stood there undecided, she noticed a faint trail between the two forks of the road, starting almost at her feet. It reminded her of the winding path Rose had worn going into the woods every morning to forage. MaryJake and Adder had followed that same path at day's end in search of her. MaryJake decided to set her feet on this faint trail, which led into a thick forest of hardwoods and pines. Her face twisted in a grin. She hadn't been forbidden to go this way, so she was still her parents' obedient child. She took a firmer grip on her bundle and strode forward.

The farther she went, and the faster she walked away from the paved road, the more the numbness wore off her feelings and rage took its place. If her thoughts had taken visible form they would have burned up the forest in one blast. Her parents had thrown her away and kept her two brothers! They loved the boys best! Thinking back, MaryJake could see they had made that clear all along. Ma, who had had schooling, was forever onto MaryJake, correcting how she spoke, how she walked, how she sat at the table. But she never once objected to how Pa and the boys mangled the language, or to their rude behavior, spitting off the porch or belching during mealtimes. When MaryJake pointed that out, Ma said, "You'll be going out into the world. You must speak well and be mannerly to make yourself acceptable. Now, hold up your shoulders."

Pa was always bragging on the boys, how much they looked like him. "Chips off the ole block," he said. And look at how they named us, she thought. Who wouldn't respect a David, a Paul? But a MaryJake is a joke, especially a MaryJake with the last name of Wildsmith. MaryJake's a name for a mule. Ma's name, Adelia—now there was a poetic name.

She hobbled into a clearing and rested on her bundle to take off her shoes. Her feet were an angry red and blistered. Close by she noticed an enormous stump, as big around as three washtubs. She limped to it for a closer look. Just as she had hoped, the stump was hollow and filled with water. Oh, to soak her worn-out feet in that water! She dipped her fingers in and smelled them. Black walnut, her nose told her. This stump had once been the base of a giant black walnut tree. MaryJake bent over, looking at her reflection—white face, white hair—in the dark brown water. She thought about how folks believed that if you ducked your head in oak stump water, your straight hair would grow out curly. She had always wanted to try it, but Ma forbade it, and besides, oak stump water stunk sour.

She trailed her fingers through the water, then felt the depth of it. Why not soak her feet? Why not soak her head and give herself curly hair? She looked at her hands, dyed brown halfway to the elbows. She couldn't fool with this stuff as long as she wore Ma's leafy green dress. It would get splotched with the rich brown color, which would never wash out, as MaryJake knew; she had helped Ma color quilt linings with black walnut dye.

She wiped her hands on a patch of grass, then opened her bundle and brought out her overalls and shirt. Folding the green dress carefully, she stashed it in the bundle. As she took off her bloomers and folded them, she thought, Why stop at turning my hair brown and curly? Why not put my whole self in the dye pot and see what happens?

The stump made a fine bathtub, though a little rough to sit in. MaryJake could lie down in it if she curled herself just right. She soaked first one side, then the other, wishing she wasn't so skinny but realizing that her thinness made the transformation easier. And she was transformed, that she could tell even from the dark mirror of the stump water after she'd climbed out and dried herself in a patch of sunlight. She redressed, welcoming the familiar comfort of her overalls and loose shirt. How glad her feet were to be released from those shoes! She tossed them into the bushes, hoping never to see them again. Before retying the bundle, she tucked Ma's handkerchief in the middle of it. She tied the faded red sash that went with her old dress around her thick wet hair to hold it off her forehead.

She took up the trail again, noticing that the sun was well down the sky toward setting. At the far edge of the clearing she came upon a graveyard with a rusty iron fence around it. Pink roses bloomed in the briars that ran wild. MaryJake hung over the fence, thinking, I ought to die here and now just to spite them. She forced open the fancy gate and went inside. Eleven graves had tombstones up-standing, and one had been turned over flat. Several other graves were marked head and foot with gritty brown rocks. MaryJake knew which was the head because bodies were buried facing east, ready to spring up when the trumpet sounded on Judgment Day. The inscriptions on the old stones suited the way she felt. Baby graves had the short-est: "A bud unbloomed," "Gone too soon." She lingered over a longer poem, wishing she could take it with her in her head:

> Come good, come woe,
> It all must end, and lives here rudely riven
> Will have their golden cords restrung
> By Angel hands in Heaven.

She wanted a pretty epitaph like that, but she knew what her folks would engrave on her tombstone: "She was an obedient child." Just for that, she wouldn't die. Nor would she be an obedient child. She flung herself out of the graveyard and went on her way.

Surely somebody had a house on this trail. She had to find it before dark. MaryJake didn't know how she would explain herself, but she didn't want to spend the night in the woods. And her stomach grumbled for food.

SEVEN

S HE HADN'T GONE FAR when she began hearing a barnyard uproar. She forgot her anger as she puzzled over what could be happening. The noise reminded her of the animals who ran away to Bremen in the story she often told her brothers. With their terrifying cries, the animals scared the robber band out of the rich house and lived happily ever after. At the end of the story, she and Paul and David always joined in a loud chorus of farm animals, trying to outdo each other, which made them fall in a heap laughing.

What MaryJake was hearing now sounded worse than any racket she and her brothers had ever made. The trail led her nearer and nearer the uproar, into the yard of a one-room house, neat but bare except for old pots and pans filled with petunia plants spilling blossoms over the sides. But the racket was not coming from the house. A nearby barn lot, enclosed by a crooked rail fence, was crowded with an assortment of animals, and all of them were hollering—turkeys gobbled, hens cackled, a donkey snorted and brayed, baby calves mooed, geese complained, and off to themselves a bunch of speckled guineas shrieked *pot-rack, pot-rack* in alarm. Two goats baaed and butted heads. Noisiest of all was a pig who kept up a continuous high-pitched whine, a hunger whine.

MaryJake knew how he felt—she was hungry herself—but she wanted to shake that pig and shout in his pink ear, "Hush up!" She stopped short of doing so because in the center of the uproar stood an old woman in a long-sleeved patched dress with an apron over it. Her hands held the apron to her face and her shoulders shook with sobs MaryJake couldn't hear.

She yelled, "Hey, lady! Ma'am! What's the matter?" but her voice wouldn't rise above the noise. MaryJake couldn't see the gate into the enclosure so she laid down her bundle and climbed over the rails. Some of the animals quieted as she came in their midst, but others stared at her and hollered louder. When MaryJake touched the woman's arm, she looked up with tears pouring out of her loose-rimmed eyes.

"Help you?" MaryJake shouted.

The woman wiped her face. "They want supper," her quavering voice said in MaryJake's ear. "But we can't get . . . food. . . . A booger-bear . . . scared. . . ." She pointed a trembling finger at the open barn door and began crying again.

MaryJake couldn't see a scary thing, but she didn't want to get any closer without a club. She took a half-rotted rail off the top of the fence and warily stepped inside the wide barn opening. She saw no booger-bear, but the feed room and animal stalls on either side of her gradually took shape. As her eyes adjusted to the shadows, she saw, coiled on the ground in front of her, the biggest snake she had ever faced. Not only was its thick body coiled round in a pile, but nearly a foot of it was raised straight up in the air. Its neck had widened out flat, its head was hooded, and it hissed like a deadly cobra. MaryJake stood dumb for a minute, not moving. Then she laughed, though she had been sure a moment before that she would never laugh again. "You fooler!" she said. "You puffing adder!"

She advanced upon it, poking it gently with the rail. The snake collapsed and thrashed about on the ground, its mouth open and its tongue hanging out in a most dreadful way. MaryJake, knowing it was putting on a show to scare her away, continued poking the rail at it until it rolled over on its back and lay as if dead. Taking a secure hold behind the snake's jaws and supporting the heavy muscular body with her other hand, she brought it out of the barn. The animals scattered ahead of her. At the fence she carefully pushed the snake through an opening between rails into a patch of weeds. Replacing her weapon on top of the fence, she turned to the old woman. "It's only an old puffing adder. Nothing to fear. He keeps the bad snakes away."

The animals quieted down. Two silent peafowls joined the group, raising each foot high, then setting it down deliberately. Their long tails, folded like a lady's fancy fan, had golden eyes on them. MaryJake thought them a peaceful addition to the other loud-mouthed beggars.

"I'll help you feed," she offered.

The old woman dried her eyes. She showed MaryJake which animals went into what stalls and where the poultry roosted for the night.

"After the pot-racks eat, they sleep in the trees, and so do the peafowls," she said over the sound of grain falling into feed troughs and the rustling of hay.

The pig—the old woman addressed him as Culver—stayed in a shelter that leaned against the side of the barn near the door. The last thing, MaryJake climbed into the loft and threw down straw for the beds.

Standing in the barn door with the old woman, facing the creatures inside, listening to the chomping and the contented sighs, and smelling the sweet hay and grain, MaryJake felt almost happy.

"It's summertime," she said. "Why do you keep your critters in at night?"

The old woman looked solemn and lowered her voice. "It's the varmint. He lives down on the creek and prowls around my house at night, hunting for a tasty supper."

"What kind of varmint?"

"A bad varmint. In one night he stole Culver's mama and all Culver's brothers and sisters." They stopped at the pig's pen and she bent down to scratch his head. "Only reason he didn't get Culver is I had him in the house for doctoring that night. He got well and is growing up to be a fine boy, he is." Culver made agreeing noises in his throat and curled his pink tail tighter.

The old woman looked MaryJake up and down. "You're a fine boy too. How did you know me and my animals needed you at this particular time?"

MaryJake was caught short: the old lady took her for a boy. That's fine—I'll be a boy, MaryJake thought, casting her mind around for a way to account for her sudden appearance. She pitched her voice lower and drawled her words. "Ummmm—yessum, I kinda growed up with animals and snakes and thangs. Being my pa's onliest boy, I had to learn to work with him." Listening to herself was like hearing Pa talk. Mustn't overdo it, she thought, afraid she'd give herself away.

The old woman went ahead of MaryJake out of the barnyard and fastened the rails together securely. "What you doing in the woods by yourself? And so late in the day? Nobody takes this path—it don't come from anywhere and it don't go nowhere."

"Well," MaryJake said, "I'm kinda lost, I guess. My folks sent me away, them being so poor and us having the Depression. I was to stay with some people and earn my keep, but seems like I lost their address, and somehow I mislaid my money. If I could just stay the night with you maybe?" At least part of what she said was true. She crossed her fingers on the rest.

"Sure 'nuff," the old woman said. "Come on in, and let's eat a bite. You can tell me the name o'them people. If they live hereabouts, I ought to have heerd of 'em."

EIGHT

WHILE THEY PAUSED at the wash pan and the water bucket on the porch shelf, a terrible yelp came from the barn. MaryJake dropped the homemade soap bar and stood transfixed as the cry was repeated over and over, like an anguished woman set upon by thieves who were tearing her apart.

"It's nothing," the old woman said. "Just the King of Sheba going to bed. That's the peafowl, the male. Him and the Queen of Sheba roost on the low limb of that oak by the barn."

The penetrating cries continued, battering MaryJake's eardrums.

"He'll stop in a while. Seems like that's his way of saying good night to the world."

"Every night?" MaryJake gasped.

"Ever' night, as sure as sundown."

MaryJake shuddered at the thought of hearing that yelping every night. It was all the more terrible because those two peafowls had acted like the most peaceable critters in the whole barnyard! She drank a dipperful of water from the bucket. She drank another, realizing she hadn't had a drop of water this livelong day. She sloshed water out of the pan over her face and dried on the towel hanging from a nail on the post.

"I don't want to be a bit of trouble to you," MaryJake said, following the old woman inside. She could barely see her in the shadowed cabin. The old woman turned up the wick of the kerosene lamp and lit it.

"I'm Miz Bennett—Mary Bennett. I'm a widow woman. Been living here since I wuz borned. And what name are you called by?"

MaryJake glanced around the room, at the stacked-up clutter from years back, the old chairs, and the bare floor, while she planned her answer. "My name's Jake," she finally said. "Jake Smith." Making secure her identify as a boy and taming down her last name gave MaryJake a strange satisfaction.

"I kinda thought you might be a gypsy boy, wearing that red band 'round your head that way. You're brown as a gypsy too. And I bet those cat-green eyes o'yours can see clear into the middle o'next week." She was opening the door to a pie safe in the corner and setting out small dishes while she talked. "But Smith's not a gypsy name. Besides, no gypsies've been anywhere near here in a long time. I'm too po' for them to make money off'n me, and I sure don't need my fortune told." She laughed. When she lifted the covers off the food, MaryJake saw cornbread, green beans, fried green tomatoes, and several slices of cheese. "Hep yourself," Miz Bennett said.

MaryJake took second helpings on everything. She ate

till she thought she would burst. Miz Bennett could hardly eat for watching MaryJake, and she kept smiling. "I forgot what it wuz like to have a boy 'round to make the food disappear. You sure know how to eat."

MaryJake didn't mention that she hadn't eaten since before sunup. "You're an almighty good cook," she said as she sopped up the bean juice in her plate with the last piece of cornbread. "What time do you get up of a morning?"

"Daybreak," Miz Bennett said. Her smile drooped. "You think you'll be on your way by then?"

"How'd it be if I hang around a few days? See if I remember the name of those folks where I'm supposed to go." MaryJake sounded like Pa negotiating a sale.

"Won't they be lookin' for you? They'll be mighty worried if you don't get there."

"Oh no, ma'am. They don't know just when I'm coming."

That seemed to settle Miz Bennett's worries for the time being. MaryJake hadn't noticed when the peafowl stopped yelling, so maybe it was something she could get used to, she thought. They finished supper in pleasant silence and washed up the dishes in cold water and home-made soap. MaryJake felt so tired she couldn't keep from yawning.

Miz Bennett brought out a quilt from a drawer in an old dresser. Cedar shavings fell out as she unfolded it. "We'll spread this on the floor for your pallet. And I'll give you one of my goose-feather pillows. You'll be all right?"

"Yes, ma'am." MaryJake stared at the quilt. She had helped Ma piece quilts, and she had seen Miss Celestine's quilts, but never a quilt as beautiful as this one with tiny, tiny pieces of many bright colors swirling from all four corners and meeting in the middle like an exploding skyrocket.

Miz Bennett must have misread her amazement because she said apologetically, "Hope it's not so loud it keeps you awake. That's what my ole man said, but he always laughed. He had a jokey way 'bout him."

"What is it?" MaryJake asked, knowing that a boy would not have gone speechless over a quilt and wouldn't give a plugged nickel for its name. Careful, she thought.

"I made it up," Miz Bennett said, stroking the colored pieces with her crooked fingers. "I wanted it like the waterfall that useter be on the creek. Rainbow Falls, we called it. And see here, in each corner I put one of those pretty little parrot birds that once lived in our woods. Truth is, they're the ones gave our creek its name—Yellow Bird Creek, though they wuz green too. We had big flocks of 'em back then."

"Rainbow Falls on Yellow Bird Creek," MaryJake said, liking the picture it made in her mind. A yawn took her by surprise, springing her mouth so wide open the jaw hinges cracked. She felt like collapsing on the pallet in her overalls.

Miz Bennett smiled and reached in the quilt drawer again. This time she brought out a long white shirt with a big collar. "You can sleep in this. 'Twuz my ole man's, long time ago. Now I know why I saved it." She smiled again.

MaryJake stretched out on the quilt, which smelled like a green cedar forest. The white shirt of Mr. Bennett's felt soft on her clean brown skin. Her stomach was well filled and comfortable. She was glad to be safe in Miz Bennett's little house and happy knowing the animals out in the barn were well fed and safe too. Miz Bennett knelt beside her bed, her knee joints creaking as loud as ole Dink's, and said her prayers. Then she blew out the lamp.

MaryJake thought she'd fall asleep right away from tiredness and her sore feet, but she didn't. She said her prayers because she was thankful not to be alone out in the night with the varmint Miz Bennett said lurked in the woods. She refused to think about Ma and Pa but she missed her little brothers. Her life and theirs had been "rudely riven," but she hoped she wouldn't have to wait for heaven to see them again.

She named over each wildflower her brothers had picked to soothe her grief over Adder: may apple, sweet shrub, windflower, thimbleweed, meadow rue, bugbane, bouncing bet, Adam-and-Eve, rose pogonia, hoary puccoon, bluebells. Was it only this morning that Ma and Pa left her? Her eyes teared up as she wondered where David and Paul slept tonight—beside some dirt road or under some bridge? Were they hungry? Had the hot midday sun burned them as they rode west in the topless Model T? Where was Adder tonight? And what was the little jewel snake doing under the elephant ears? She tossed and turned, her mind unsettled.

"Jake?" Miz Bennett had to call her twice before she remembered who she was.

"Yessum?"

"Can't you sleep? Is the floor too hard?"

"No, ma'am." MaryJake made her voice sound sleepy and far away. "Ole Sandman's done sprinkled sand in my eyes. . . ."

Silence now except for the whip-poor-will that called

from deep in the woods, never pausing to draw a breath. The wind blew softly in the window, stirring the scent of cedar around the room. Gradually MaryJake was lulled to sleep on the Rainbow Falls quilt, and she dreamed about Yellow Bird Creek, where flocks of green and yellow parrots had lived.

NINE

NEXT MORNING MaryJake was up before Miz Bennett, folding her nightgown and the quilt and putting them away in the drawer. After Miz Bennett arose, dressed, and made her bed, they went to the barn to feed the animals and turn them out to rove.

"We're getting a little low on feed," Miz Bennett said. "I useter raise all the corn and hay my animals ate. But seems like old age has caught up with me."

"You buy their food?" MaryJake wondered how Miz Bennett could afford all those hungry animals. And now MaryJake had brought her own appetite to add to the others.

"I make do with my widow's pension. Mr. Bennett fought in the war—the war of 1865. He was fifteen then, and he never got over the damage it did to him."

"A Confederate soldier? Did he know General Lee?"

"He never said if he did or not that I recall. He walked home from Virginny, I know that. Skin and bones, he wuz, 'nuff to scare most anybody to death, but not me. I wuz ten year old, and I hepped to take care o'him. That wuz a long time ago."

Miz Bennett went in the house to make hoecakes for breakfast while MaryJake shoveled out the stalls and put down clean straw, thinking about Mr. Bennett and General Lee. She wished Adder could be here to keep her company. He would make short work of that varmint, whoever it was, but no use to get overwrought about Adder now.

She found a wooden wheelbarrow with a rusty metal wheel and hauled the manure to a cleared space surrounded by a tumbledown zigzag fence. She could tell it used to be a garden by the dead cornstalks and the dried up tomato vines.

After they ate, MaryJake made two trips to the spring to bring their day's supply of water. The spring was a wonder. MaryJake liked it much better than a well. Wells, closed in and deep and dark, were scary, but the spring was in open shade. The water was so clear it had a blue cast, and it boiled up out of white sand in the bottom of a hollow log and then rushed away downhill.

MaryJake busied herself sweeping the one room and the porch.

Miz Bennett said, "I 'mirate how handy you are with a broom. Most boys wouldn't touch a broom with a ten-foot pole."

"I always had to help in the house any way I could," MaryJake said truthfully. "Seemed like Ma never got done with her work."

Miz Bennett nodded agreement. She watered the flowers in the rusted pots and pans on the shelf and the edge of the porch, talking to them and pinching off the dead blossoms as she went along.

MaryJake admired the way the plants grew and bloomed. "If you grow flowers so fine, why don't you have a vegetable garden?"

"Planting a garden and watching it grow is one o'the things I like best to do." Miz Bennett was silent, thinking. "I got heaps o'seed I've saved from past seasons. But I ain't no longer able to do the digging." She sank down on the step and fanned herself with her apron.

MaryJake sat down beside her and forced herself to speak in an offhand way. "While I'm trying to remember where I'm s'pose to go, why don't we make you a garden? I'll dig, you'll plant, and after that there'll only be weeding to do."

"And harvesting—that's the best part." Miz Bennett smacked her lips.

MaryJake found the digging fork in the barn and began mixing the manure into the dirt of the garden while Miz Bennett searched her house for the seeds she had saved. They worked till midday, choosing to plant their favorites. For MaryJake it was okra and watermelons. For Miz Bennett it was corn, which she called "roastnears," and tomatoes.

"We'll grow lots of purple hull peas too," Miz Bennett said. "Deers love to eat purple hulls. Maybe if we plant 'em all the way around the outside o'the fence, they won't eat our other vegetables."

"We'll patch the fence," MaryJake suggested.

"The deers won't pay attention to it—they'll jump right over. Maybe those purple hulls will keep 'em occupied long 'nuff for the corn to get ripe. But pshaw, I'm forgetting the raccoons." She laughed. "Here we've got a bare stretch o'ground and already I'm worrying over the deers and the coons."

MaryJake laughed too, but later that day she went around the fence restacking the rails that had fallen down and cutting saplings from the woods to replace the missing rails.

Miz Bennett's animals all came home about sundown from wherever they had spent the day. They gathered in the barnyard ready to eat supper and to be put to bed.

"We oughten to feed those guineas a bite," Miz Bennett said, glaring at them as they ate with the chickens and the geese and the turkeys. "They won't lay in a reg'lar nest. They hide out so I can't find their eggs, else we could have eggs ever'day."

"I'm real fond of eggs," MaryJake said. "Why don't the hens and the others lay?"

"I reckon they're molting right now—see how their feathers is missing? They'll start in again when their new feathers come out."

"Soon as we finish with the garden, I'll go guinea nest hunting."

Miz Bennett peered at her anxiously. "What 'bout those folks you're going to see? Won't they be getting worried? Or your ma and pa?"

"No, ma'am. They know I'm all right. Why, my pa says I'm as handy as a hip pocket." He had never said such a thing, but MaryJake wished he had.

"I saw that right off," Miz Bennett said, her eyes beaming. "I just wish you could live here with me forever and a day." She shook her head to get rid of the wish. "But you belong somewhere else."

"Well, one day soon I'll go nest hunting. Then maybe the rain will come to make our seeds grow. How about that for now?"

All Miz Bennett said was, "Finding a nest won't be easy. Guineas are sly." But MaryJake could tell she was pleased.

In the mornings while she did chores, MaryJake tried to keep her eyes on the guineas to see which way they went. But the flock broke up and wandered off in all directions, eating bugs and worms and making satisfied little noises to themselves. The chickens stayed together, scratching and running about the yard. The turkeys tottered about in the underbrush, lifting their feet high as they walked in and out. The donkey and Culver went off toward the spring where they spent the day in the brush.

The two goats had an appetite for Miz Bennett's petunias in the pans on the porch but a peach tree switch hung on a nail by the steps for whipping them away. It took only a whip or two to make them leap down the steps and run off thrashing their short tails angrily. The baby calves were still too young to be let out of the barnyard; they stayed in except when Miz Bennett brought them under the trees to play. She guarded them until they wore themselves out and wanted to go back into the barn lot.

MaryJake thought the peafowls' names—the King and Queen of Sheba—suited them because they looked so majestic. They walked around quietly, lifting their feet high and taking deliberate steps, and caused no difficulty till after sundown. Then the awful yelling began. Occasionally

MaryJake found a long feather on the ground, lost out of the male's tail. It looked like a royal jewel of gold and sapphire blue. How beautiful it was! She made a bouquet of peafowl feathers in a clay jug on the porch.

The geese gave MaryJake the most trouble. When she stooped over to dip feed out of a sack or turned her back for a moment to shovel manure into the wheelbarrow, one or the other of the geese stretched out a long neck, took a big bite of MaryJake through the thinnest part of her overalls, and twisted hard. "Ow!" MaryJake couldn't help hollering. She tried to keep a safe distance from them but they liked to crowd her, especially when she was not serving their supper fast enough to please them. Shooing them away made no difference.

TEN

ON THE DAY MARYJAKE decided to go nest searching, she found a basket hanging from a nail in the barn and set off up the ridge. She watched for a hollow log or a plum thicket or some other likely place that a nest might be. But she found no clue. The guineas, it seemed, had disappeared from the face of the earth.

Finally she decided to sit down under a tree and listen for their *pot-rack* calls. She hadn't been there long when she heard cow steps coming along from higher up the ridge. The steps weren't those of a cow meandering in the woods finding food or passing the time. They were purposeful steps, moving right along toward some destination.

Soon into view came the funniest sight MaryJake ever saw—a half-grown black-and-white-spotted calf with a half-grown red-headed girl mounted astride him. She rode bareback, her scratched and bug-bitten legs and narrow calloused feet dangling loose from underneath her ragged dress. In her right hand she held one rope rein, which was attached to the big calf's halter. In her left hand she balanced a basket of eggs, large brown freckled eggs. As she jounced along she sang a song MaryJake had heard Ma sing, a play-party song about King George's son William, who wore a star on his breast. The girl had come to the part that said:

> *Go choose yore east, go choose yore west,*
> *Choose the one that you loooove best.*
> *If he's not heeere to take his paaart,*
> *Choose the one next in yore heaaart.*

Ma hadn't pronounced the words in that drawn-out way, forcing them through her nose, but MaryJake liked hearing the familiar song. If she hadn't been startled out of her mind by the sight, she would have burst out laughing. As it was she sat without moving until the calf saw her and stopped suddenly. The girl didn't notice MaryJake right away. She continued singing, using her heels to urge the big-eyed calf to move forward. When he humped his back and bawled a refusal, the girl saw what was scaring him. Now it was her turn to be startled. The song choked off. Her eyes bugged out. Her jaw dropped, revealing decayed front teeth. Her freckled nose wrinkled in a nervous twitch, and her bright red hair corkscrewed in every direction. MaryJake had never in her life seen such a homely, plumb ugly person. She was as ugly as a mud fence stuck full of spider legs. Immediately she felt sorry for that thought and stood up.

"It's only me," she said, hoping the girl would look better when she wasn't so scared. "I'm hunting guinea nests." She toed her basket toward the calf to prove her claim.

"Well, you don't have to scare anybody to death. You nearly made me drop Granny's eggs. Then I would have been in a fix for sure." She inspected MaryJake with quick brown eyes. "You're not anybody I ever saw before."

"Neither are you. Where are you headed?"

"To the store to put the eggs on our bill. And the post office. My granny's expecting a letter."

"Whereabouts are the store and the post office?" MaryJake asked.

"They're in the settlement, boy, where the big rock castle is. Ain't you seen the rock castle?" She sounded proud, as if it belonged to her. The calf meantime stretched his short neck to reach a clump of grass.

MaryJake wanted to keep this girl talking a while longer. "Your calf looks like he needs to rest in the shade and eat a bite."

"He needs a drink of water. We'll go by the spring down the hill a ways."

MaryJake walked beside them to Miz Bennett's spring where the girl slid off the calf's back, being careful with the basket. She threw the rein over his neck and let him stand in the stream and drink while she cupped her hands under the water running over the rim of the hollow log for her own drink. "This is the best water anywhere," she said, smoothing her hair down with her wet hands. "Where you live?"

"Over there." MaryJake nodded toward Miz Bennett's place, which was hidden by a little wooded rise.

"Is she your grandma?" the girl asked.

"Sorta. Where's your house?"

The girl pointed back the way she had come. "Up on the ridge. My name's Hannah Mowry. The boys at school call me Hannah Meow-ry, but I don't care."

"You go to school?" MaryJake hadn't thought about a school being anywhere near.

"Sometimes. 'Cept when I've got the toothache." She was wading in the water now, cooling her feet. "When my teeth ache, I hurt all over. 'Specially the roots o'my hair." The girl shuddered.

MaryJake looked at her tangled bushy head and thought about each of those fiery hairs hurting. That must be real pain.

Hannah said, "You didn't say your name."

"Jake Smith. I'm going to build a toadfrog house." MaryJake sat on the stream bank and patted the wet sand over the front half of her foot. Hannah watched MaryJake as she carefully inched her foot out, leaving an igloo-shaped sand house. "See. Just the right size for a toadfrog."

"I'm going to make one—only one," Hannah decided. "Then I got to go. I have to be home before dark. I'm skeered o'the varmint."

"The varmint?"

"That moon-eyed boy. He lives down on the creek, Uncle George says. He prowls at night 'cause the sun is pizen to him. One little ray'll kill him deader'n hell, Uncle George says. And he's a top-notch thief. He makes off with anything that suits his fancy."

"He better not come around Miz Bennett's," MaryJake said.

"He's already been there, a hunderd times, stole her nearly 'bout blind, Uncle George says."

MaryJake filed that information in her mind for future consideration, then asked, "What's your calf's name?"

"Buck. Learned him myself. Want to ride him sometime?"

"I never rode a calf. Will he pull a wagon?"

"Yep. Uncle George made him a real fine cart." A shadow passed over Hannah's face. Then she stood up, dusted the sand off her dress, and called Buck. He came as obediently as a dog. She remounted, MaryJake handed her the basket of eggs, and Hannah started Buck downhill again. Over her shoulder she called, "I'll come down in the morning and help you hunt guinea nests."

"I'll be here." MaryJake waved till Hannah rode out of sight.

As she washed the sand off her hands and feet, she recognized mint growing in the shade on the far bank. She crushed one of the velvet-soft leaves and took a deep breath. Nothing smelled so clean as mint, unless it was pine straw or cedar shavings. She picked the tenderest sprigs, rinsed them under the spring overflow, and laid them in her basket. When she returned to the house, she found Miz Bennett sitting on the front porch in her old rocking chair. She didn't seem disappointed that MaryJake brought mint leaves instead of guinea eggs.

"We'll have a cup of tea this minute," Miz Bennett said.

She filled the kettle and set it over the flame of the kerosene stove while MaryJake got out the cups and saucers. Miz Bennett's teakettle made MaryJake laugh. Every time just before it came to a boil it gave a scream like a red-tailed hawk, warning everybody to get ready to do whatever they needed to with the hot water.

While they sat on the porch inhaling the fragrance

of their tea, waiting for it to cool enough for drinking, MaryJake told Miz Bennett about meeting Hannah Mowry.

"Hannah's a smart girl, a real crackerjack. But her uncle George is a heartbreaker. Trouble's his middle name. Bad trouble."

"But he made Buck a cart to pull," MaryJake protested.

"He'll charm the horns off a billy goat. He's not home right now. He got caught making whiskey and the judge sent him off."

George, in the penitentiary. His letter would be the one Hannah's grandma hoped for. MaryJake thought a little prayer: Please don't let Hannah be disappointed. But what if George didn't know how to write? MaryJake quickly enlarged her prayer: Please make George know how to write.

"Moonshining is what most ever'body does up on the ridge," Miz Bennett continued. "If they didn't, I reckon they'd all starve to death."

MaryJake took a long drink of the mint tea that cooled her at the same time as it burned her throat. Seems like everybody struggles every minute of the day to keep from starving, she thought. That was the way it had been with Ma and Pa too. Keeping the young'uns fed year round and warm in the winter was what powered every day, but she was sure that Pa never had anything to do with making whiskey. Both her parents believed drunkenness was a Great Evil, and they talked hard against it. She did not know what to make of Hannah living with a bunch of moonshiners.

"Who has money to buy moonshine?" MaryJake wondered aloud.

"Mostly folks from town, boys from the university," Miz Bennett said. "They're the folks with cars to haul it."

"Is the varmint a whiskey maker?"

"Not him. He don't make it nor drink it, according to what I heerd. Stealing's his vice. He steals far and wide."

MaryJake glanced around the yard and shivered. "He might be watching us now."

"No need to fear him in the daylight. He wouldn't dare set foot outside till dark on account o'him being moon-eyed or somethin'."

MaryJake put together what Hannah and Miz Bennett told her about the varmint and formed an awful picture of a clammy white toadstool with clutching fingers and eyes shaped like full moons. She hoped he wouldn't show up in her dreams.

ELEVEN

H ANNAH AND BUCK were waiting when MaryJake came in sight of the spring next morning. "You know what?" Hannah shouted. "On my way home yestiddy, there was a toadfrog in your house!"

MaryJake grinned. "I didn't know they truly lived in a house. Let's build some more."

As they slipped their feet in and out of the damp sand houses, Hannah said, "Wouldn't it be hateful to have to wear shoes? We couldn't build houses."

"Nor wade in the branch," MaryJake said. "Nor shinny up a tree where there ain't no limbs."

They built in silence for a time, then MaryJake said in an offhand way, "Did your granny's letter come?"

"What letter?" Hannah concentrated on rebuilding a house that collapsed when she pulled her foot out of it.

"Any letter," MaryJake said, not wanting to hem her in.

"No letter yet for anybody."

MaryJake tried to keep her voice from sounding sympathetic. "Maybe next time."

"Sure 'nuff," was all Hannah said, but she made it plain that she didn't want any pity.

When they started on the nest hunt, they left a row of sand houses along each bank of the stream. Looking back, MaryJake said, "They're not just for toadfrogs. Let's allow anything to live in them that wants to."

"That's right. Anybody who'll fit." Hannah took off Buck's halter and hung it on a branch. "Now you eat till we come back," she instructed the calf. She turned to MaryJake. "Did you know cows don't have upper teeth? That's funny to me. Just teeth on the bottom of their mouths. How can they chew?"

"Cows do have upper teeth," MaryJake insisted. "In the back of their mouths."

Hannah shook her head. "I've had my hand in Buck's mouth lots o'times when he was a baby calf. Once he got choked on a rag he wuz chewing and I had to pull it out. He didn't have any upper teeth."

"Will he let you look now?" MaryJake studied Buck's big mouth doubtfully.

Hannah patted the calf on his hornless head. "Buck buddy, I'm gonna see about your teeth." She stroked his jaw and pulled down his lower lip. "Look at his fine teeth. He never has a toothache. If only my teeth could be like his." She wedged his mouth open with her fingers, shoved her hand in the back, and felt his upper jaw. "Sure 'nuff! You got teeth up there—big hard teeth." Hannah sounded accusing, as if he had been keeping a secret from her. Buck wasn't bothered; he slobbered over her hand, licking her fingers. "That's how I learned him to drink milk," she explained, wiping her hand on her dress. "He didn't have no ma. I'd dip my fingers in a bucket o'warm milk to learn him how to suck. Then he found out he could get more milk faster if he stuck his nose in the bucket and drank. And that wuz what I wanted him to do all along."

Buck followed them through the bushes until he found a patch of grass big enough so he could settle in and eat a while. MaryJake watched him gathering the green blades in his wide mouth with his tongue and pulling them off with a jerk of his head. Her throat ached from her remembering Rose. She knew how Hannah felt about Buck.

The two of them searched in half circles, making each one larger than the last. They hadn't found any sign of a guinea nest when they came to a rock jutting out over a hollow. Across the hollow, halfway along the brow of a low hill, a party of people appeared to be picking berries, but MaryJake knew no berries were ripe yet. She stared at the figures. None of them moved. They seemed frozen in motion.

Hannah glanced back to see why she had stopped. MaryJake pointed, unable to say a word. Hannah shrugged. "It's nothing," she said. "Uncle George did it."

"Who are they?"

"Nobody," Hannah said, turning her back on them. "Uncle George fixed them."

MaryJake could see a woman who wore a dress down to her ankles with long sleeves. Her bonnet hid her face and hair. The man had on overalls and a shirt. His ragged straw hat shaded his face. MaryJake could count four children, more or less. They were partially hidden by the bushes. "Come on. Let's go over there. I want to see them up close." She started down the hillside.

Hannah seized her arm. "No, Jake. No. Don't go anywhere near them."

MaryJake tried to pull free. "I want to see them close."

"If you knew my uncle George, you'd stay as far away as you could."

Hannah's voice had such a scary sound to it that MaryJake stopped resisting and looked at her. "Why did he do it?"

Hannah turned away without answering.

"I don't understand." MaryJake protested. Then in a flash she realized this make-believe family must have been put there to guard George's still. A lawman or anybody else seeing those berry pickers from a distance would think there was no whiskey still anywhere near.

MaryJake followed Hannah slowly, looking back now and then at the strange sight across the hollow. Even though she knew meddling in a moonshiner's whiskey still was dangerous, she tried to fix in her mind where this place was so she could find it again. But the zigzag way Hannah led through the brush soon caused MaryJake to lose her bearings. She noticed how dejected Hannah looked. Maybe it was time to end the nest hunt.

"I'm tired," MaryJake called. "Let's go find Buck."

"Fine with me," Hannah said, and they headed straight up the hill. Near the top of the hill, not far from the spring, they found the guinea nest in a clump of blackberry brambles.

MaryJake laughed. "We found it when we weren't looking!"

"It found us, I think!" Hannah said. "Look at all the eggs!"

They knelt down, reaching carefully through the briars

to bring the small speckled eggs out one by one. When the eggs covered the bottom of the basket, Hannah snapped off cool green leaves to lay over them. Then they made another layer of eggs, covered it, and yet another.

"Thirty-five!" MaryJake said when they finished. "What a prize!"

"Oughten we to leave one for a nest egg?" Hannah asked. "Now we know where the nest is, we want them to keep laying in it."

MaryJake saw the good sense of that and replaced an egg in the nest. "But guineas are so particular, I doubt they'll come back. I bet they're watching us now." She looked all around but couldn't see any of the black-and-white speckled fowl.

Back at the spring, they found Buck lying in the shade, chewing his cud. Hannah rousted him up, haltered him, and mounted.

MaryJake called to mind the eggs Hannah had taken to the store yesterday to pay on their bill. She doubted Hannah's family had any eggs left to eat themselves but she knew she had to be careful in the way she offered to give Hannah some.

"You ever eat guinea eggs?" she asked. When Hannah shook her head, MaryJake took a dozen from under the cool leaves. "You and your grandma try these. See if they're worth our hard work."

Hannah drew back. MaryJake thought she was going to refuse, but then she cupped her hands to make a bowl. "Granny will like them," she said smiling down at the eggs. Then she nudged Buck into a trot up toward the ridge, letting his rein dangle.

TWELVE

A SOAKING RAIN CAME, then the sun shone warm for a few days, and Miz Bennett's garden sprang out of the ground. Every day before sunset when chores were done, MaryJake and Miz Bennett hung over the rail fence, admiring the seedlings.

"I do believe ever' single seed sprouted," Miz Bennett said.

MaryJake agreed. "We'll have to sharpen our hoes and get ready for the weeds."

It was at such a time Hannah and Buck rode into the yard on their way home. Hannah was carrying a can of kerosene in a gunnysack across Buck's back. MaryJake could smell it.

"Can you meet me tomorrow?" she asked MaryJake, after greeting them. "I got a surprise for you."

Miz Bennett smiled. "A play-pretty?"

Hannah laughed showing her snaggle teeth. "Jake might not think it's a play-pretty. I'll wait at the spring, early." And she hurried off into the twilight.

MaryJake puzzled and puzzled over Hannah's surprise, but it was all wasted effort because she never came near to guessing it. When she arrived at the spring next morning Hannah was there on Buck and holding a rope attached to a white calf slightly larger than Buck. MaryJake threw up her hands in astonishment. Hannah laughed so hard she doubled over Buck's head and dropped his rein though she held onto the white cow. When she could talk she gasped, "You look like you seed a ghost."

MaryJake came up to the white stranger slowly. When he didn't back away, she scratched him along his backbone and under his chin. He stretched out his neck, telling her to scratch more. "Who is it?" she asked as she patted and scratched.

"Bennie. And he can plow good as a mule. But I've been learning him about riding so you can go with me and Buck."

"Where do you and Buck go?" MaryJake asked. "Besides the settlement."

"Well, that's somethin' I want to talk to you about. But I couldn't tell you in front of Miz Bennett, 'cause she might not like it."

"I'm all ears," MaryJake said, wondering what was coming.

Hannah dismounted and leaned over to check Buck's hoof. She was having a hard time saying whatever she wanted to say.

MaryJake was impatient. "You want me to go somewhere with you?"

"Nope. Yep. Oh, Jake, I'm skeered you'll be mad."

"Tell me. Can't nothing make me mad."

"Well," Hannah said. "I wondered if you want to go in business with me. Be my partner."

"What kind of business?" MaryJake was more than ever astonished.

"Makin' money. I sell things. See this tow sack?" The rough woven bag lay across Buck's shoulders. "I put what I find in here. Then I sell it."

"You mean junk? Stuff like that?"

"Naw. Not junk." Hannah blushed. "Whiskey bottles."

MaryJake couldn't understand. "Whiskey's not legal in this county."

"I know this is a dry county," Hannah said primly.

"You find whiskey bottles? Whereabouts?"

"I ride Buck along the highway where people passin' by throw out whiskey bottles. They buy 'em in a wet county. Or up north. People from up north throw out the best bottles—they drink store-bought whiskey on their way to Florida."

"How do you make money off throwaway whiskey bottles?"

"My uncle George. He gives me a nickel apiece for ever' boughten whiskey bottle I find. And I look good for 'em, down in the ditches on both sides o'the highway and over in the bushes. He gives me three cents for every common jar I find—anything glass. He gives a penny to boot if there's a lid."

MaryJake knew better than to ask her what filled the bottles. Uncle George's homemade whiskey, she was sure. And she had become ever more sure that those imitation people on the hillside were George's way of throwing the law off his trail. Her thoughts went back to Ma and Pa and how they hated strong drink. Pa said intoxicants made men mistreat their children, but as MaryJake saw the matter, some men didn't need whiskey to make them do that.

She was silent for so long Hannah became worried. "You can't tell anybody, now, you hear? Not Miz Bennett, not a soul!"

MaryJake wasn't thinking of telling anybody. She was staggered at the possibility of having money of her own. She had never even thought about such a possibility. But now, maybe, maybe, . . . She gulped a deep breath, grinned at Hannah, and said, "Sure 'nuff! I'll partner you!"

Learning to ride Bennie was fun by itself. He was a little slow, but after Hannah taught MaryJake about being patient with him, they got along fine. He understood "gee," meaning to the right, and "haw," to the left, "giddyup" and "whoa," and that was about all he needed to know.

"He won't trot the way Buck does," Hannah said. "That's 'cause he's always pulled a plow, and you never trot pulling a plow."

MaryJake practiced riding Bennie near the spring several times before they took the tow sack and rode out to the paved road. Hannah made her own trail through the woods, but they still came out where MaryJake's parents had left her. MaryJake deliberately rode Bennie over the exact spot where she had stood watching her family drive away. How could there be no sign of what had happened here? She bit her tongue to keep the tears out of her eyes and made herself remember what it was she wanted to ask Hannah. "That road to the right. Where does it go?"

"Up to where I live. The ridge."

So it was the ridge that Ma warned her against. Ma

knew what was up there. Could Ma have come from around here to begin with? If so, what a laugh on her that MaryJake was now friends with one of the ridge moonshiners, or at least a kinfolk of theirs. And MaryJake was out hunting bottles to put their moonshine in to sell.

MaryJake wasn't laughing though. She felt embarrassed. Everybody who passed stared at them. Some drivers honked their horns and waved. Hannah waved back. Others laughed. Buck and Bennie acted businesslike and paid no attention to the cars.

"Once a woman stopped and made a picture of us," Hannah said. "She gave me a dime too."

"I'd like that," MaryJake said. Now that she remembered the money, she forgot about people laughing at them. She began looking in the brush off both sides of the road. Searching for bottles turned out to be hard work. They dismounted every time they saw something glinting in the weeds, then remounted to ride on. Most of what they found had mud inside.

"We'll have to scrub these at the spring and dry 'em in the sun. Uncle George won't buy a dirty bottle."

For their morning's work they had a total of four whiskey bottles and two pickle jars with lids.

"More than two bits!" Hannah said laughing as they started through the woods home. "And you get half. What will you buy?"

"I don't know," MaryJake said, bewildered. Then she remembered and her mouth watered. "A banana, I think."

"I'll buy a writing tablet and a stamp so we can write—." Hannah hesitated and didn't finish. "Strawberry ice cream. I've never tasted it, have you? Any money left over, I'll get a candy bar." She sighed. "But candy pains my teeth dreadful bad."

They scrubbed the bottles shiny with sand and rinsed them in the stream from Miz Bennett's spring. Then Hannah reloaded them in the sack. "I'll set them in the sun to dry now. Uncle George can't pay for a while but I'll bring your money as soon as he does."

"That'll be lots of money," MaryJake marveled.

"Just wait till the football games start at the university. Hooooeeeee! The road's lined solid with cars, and ever'one of 'em's throwing out the *best* bottles."

THIRTEEN

MARYJAKE COULD HARDLY sleep thinking about money, money of her own to spend for whatever she wanted. Lurking at the edge of her mind like the creek varmint outside at night was the thought that with money she could start westward on the paved road and find her folks. At least find David and Paul. They would be glad to see her. She couldn't let herself think about Ma and Pa.

Something about Hannah puzzled her. However much they rode in the woods, Hannah never went near the clearing. In a way MaryJake was glad because she knew she had to redye her skin and her hair soon and she didn't want to be discovered at the job. The sun was browning her, she could tell, but at the same time it was bleaching her hair too white too quick. She had figured if she gradually let herself lighten back to normal, maybe nobody would notice. Already since she'd been here she had slipped Miz Bennett's scissors and cut her hair as best she could. By the feel she could tell the back was shaggy, but Miz Bennett had no second mirror she could use to see how to do a neater job.

Miz Bennett didn't mention MaryJake leaving anymore. Each day they did their chores, hoed the garden, and wished for more rain. Culver stopped spending the day in the brush with the donkey. He hung around MaryJake like a dog, watching her with bright little eyes that seemed to smile. Whenever MaryJake sat on the porch step, Culver lay close enough to her feet for her to scratch him with her toes. When she worked in the garden he peeked at her through a crack between the rails. He talked to her the way Katura's piglets used to do, sidling up to her to be petted or sung to. Some nights MaryJake took a tidbit of her supper out to his pen to end his day and sat with him a while. She felt safe letting herself love the chubby pink pig because she knew Miz Bennett would starve herself before she'd eat a bite of Culver.

One day Miz Bennett showed MaryJake some clean corn shucks she had stored in the barn. "We'll make a mattress for you today, how 'bout. Then you won't have to sleep on a pallet." They spread the shucks in the sun to air and Miz Bennett brought out several clean fertilizer sacks, coarsely woven with the writing almost bleached out of them, to sew together to make a bag shaped like an oversized envelope. When night came, by the light of the kerosene lamp they stuffed the sweet-smelling shucks in a slit they had left along the side of the bag, and then sewed up the slit. They laid the bag on the floor, shaking the shucks and pummeling them to make a comfortable mattress for MaryJake to sleep on. That night she had her best night's sleep since coming to Miz Bennett's cabin. In the morning

MaryJake shoved her shuck mattress under Miz Bennett's bed to stay until she needed it at nighttime.

"It's like a trundle bed," Miz Bennett said, pleased.

MaryJake continued to keep her bundle in the drawer with the rainbow quilt and the nightshirt. She had no fear that Miz Bennett would look in it. But she worried about slipping off to the black walnut stump before the water in it dried up. Miz Bennett didn't like for her to go into the woods alone. Her chance came when Miz Bennett tied on her bonnet to walk to the post office for her pension check.

"They cash my check at the store. I pay a bit on my bill and they give me a setup. A candy bar or a dope. What would you like?"

"Something you like too," MaryJake said.

"A Nehi soda pop? That's good when you're thirsty. A Grape or Orange Crush?" They agreed on an Orange Crush, which MaryJake had never tasted but it sounded good. "I'll order feed too, and chicken scratch if I can find somebody to bring it up here."

As soon as Miz Bennett left, MaryJake took a bucket of water and headed for the clearing. The dye water in the stump was low as she had suspected it would be. She added the water she had brought, stirring it around with a stick till it blended. The diluted water would not dye her as dark as before, but that was part of her plan to gradually lighten her coloring. When she climbed in the tub the water rose enough that she was able to soak herself all over and douse her hair thoroughly. She dried herself in a sunny spot the way she had the first time. As she put her shirt and overalls back on she noticed how worn they were in places.

Soon she'd have to use some precious bottle money to buy new ones.

She visited the graveyard before leaving the clearing. Her conscience hurt her a twinge to see the gate standing ajar as she had left it in her anger. The pink roses still bloomed, single petaled like a Cherokee rose. She studied her favorite inscription again, wanting to learn it well enough to tell Hannah. Thinking about Hannah, she remembered the cart Uncle George had made for Buck. Why couldn't they use it to bring home Miz Bennett's animal feed? Course, then MaryJake would have to go into the settlement to help Hannah with the delivery, and she dreaded the thought of seeing the rock castle where she was supposed to be living. She didn't want to be reminded how tangled her life had become.

MaryJake was hoeing in the garden when Miz Bennett returned carrying a brown paper bag. "I've got our setup, a sure 'nuff Orange Crush," she said. "Come in the shade and let's drink it while it's cold." Miz Bennett poured half of the orange liquid into a cup and let MaryJake drink out of the bottle. It tasted like a too sweet orange and had a zippy odor that prickled her nose.

"I ordered feed for the critters, but so far there's nobody to deliver it. Folks from the settlement don't like to come near the ridge." Miz Bennett seemed out of breath.

MaryJake drained the bottle and ran her tongue inside it, hoping for one more drop. "I'll ask Hannah. Her uncle George made a cart for Buck to pull."

"Hannah's not been around lately. Reckon she's all right?"

MaryJake had worried over Hannah's absence too.

"I'll go see about her. How do I find her place?" She spoke braver than she felt. Hannah had made it plain she didn't want MaryJake coming to the ridge.

Miz Bennett was slow in answering. "I don't know . . . if you should. We need the feed, but . . . you mustn't ever let dark catch you on the ridge." Her wrinkled lips trembled as if she wanted to say more but didn't. "The first cabin you come to after you reach the ridge—that's the Mowrys'."

MaryJake hesitated. She was anxious about Hannah, but she didn't want Miz Bennett to worry. Then, too, she wasn't a bit happy to think about going up on the ridge. Tomorrow would be a new day. Maybe Hannah and Buck would come trotting into the yard. MaryJake sighed with relief at the thought. "I'll see about going tomorrow."

Miz Bennett's face puckered. "That's dandy, Jake. There's not a bit o'hurry."

FOURTEEN

B UT HANNAH DIDN'T show up next day.
MaryJake had hardly slept a wink worrying over her,
and neither had Miz Bennett. MaryJake knew she had to
find out what was wrong. She hurried along the trail that
Hannah had come down so often on Buck. How many
days since she had seen them? At least four. Even on the
days Hannah didn't come to go riding for bottles she usually stopped by on her way to the store. Thinking about
it made MaryJake travel faster. The trail was rocky but it
didn't hinder her—her feet had calloused over the bottom
like a leather sole. Maybe she was growing hooves like
Buck and Bennie.

At the highest place, where the land leveled out for
what must be the ridge, MaryJake stopped to look around.
Here at hand the trees had been cut clear, but she could
see far distant forests and blue hills in every direction. She
had never been up so high or seen any view so beautiful.
She thought of the plenteous wildflowers that must be
growing all around with no people to see them or dig them

up or use them for doctoring. She took a last look far away and started off again.

Soon she came upon a cabin much like Miz Bennett's, the yard bare swept, a shelf with a bucket and a wash pan running the length of the porch between the posts. She knew right away it was Hannah's house because Buck and Bennie were playing in the shade of a big oak, butting heads, trying to push each other over. They stopped when she spoke to them. She could tell they recognized her—she could see the slow thoughts on their faces and in their long-lashed eyes. By the time they decided to come to her she was up on the porch calling Hannah's name.

A thin woman clasping her hands in front of her apron appeared in the door. Her clothes were splotched with grease and her hair was uncombed. She stared ahead with blank eyes. "Hanner's under the weather," she said in a faint voice. "Who's wanting her?"

"It's me, Jake. I'm wondering where she is."

"Oh, Jake. From Miz Bennett's. We did love those guinea eggs you sent."

In a sunny spot of the yard, MaryJake saw the clean bottles spread on boards, drying.

"Is she here? Can I talk to her?" Hannah's grandma seemed to grow bigger, blocking the door. "Please, ma'am."

"She's asleep," the old voice whispered.

MaryJake tried to look beyond Hannah's grandma into the dark room. She felt desperate to see Hannah. "I'll be quiet," she promised, gently squeezing past her. She made out a bed in a corner and went toward it. Before she got close enough to know if it was Hannah sprawled on the covers, she smelled something that made her nose wrinkle, a sour corn-mash odor, like pig feed that had set too long in the hot sun. Yes, it was Hannah, on her back, her eyes shut, her face swollen, breathing through her wide open mouth.

She was drunk. Every breath that came out of her mouth made MaryJake sick. She drew back. Her stomach churned up in her throat. She rushed past Hannah's grandma to the porch and fresh air. Leaning against a post, trying not to vomit, she couldn't believe what she'd seen. Cheerful, outdoor Hannah in that dark, stinking place, dead drunk.

When MaryJake could raise her head she looked at Hannah's grandma still standing at the door, her eyes unfocused. "Why? Why?" she asked, knowing she had no right to question.

But Hannah's grandma answered. "She hurts so. The aching o'her teeth—I can't stand her hurting so hard. I give her a little drink o'the backings, and then another little drink, and pretty soon she's asleep and not hurting anymore."

Oh, Hannah! Hannah! How can I help you? MaryJake thought.

Then MaryJake remembered the calves. "Can I feed Buck and Bennie? Gather your eggs?"

Hannah's grandma lifted her head, her chin jutting out. "No, thankee. I can take care o'what needs to be done." She stood proud for a minute. Then her face sort of melted. "Can you read?" she whispered.

MaryJake was so surprised she couldn't say anything.

"Can you read?" the whisper came again.

"Yes, ma'am."

Hannah's grandma pulled a wrinkled paper out of her

apron pocket. "The post office lady sent her boy with this yestiddy."

It was a letter printed on lined tablet paper. MaryJake glanced at the end and saw "Geo." printed with a flourish. "deer ma they may let me cum home," she read, squinting over some of the words. Certain letters were shaded darker as if he had chewed and wet the pencil point in his struggle to put the words on paper. When he made a mistake he scratched over it and tried again. MaryJake pictured him writing with a pencil stub that had no eraser. "i been behaving good an i tole them your blind i rote the judg to ask mercy ma don't give hanner no backings no matter how her teeth hurts i am cuming ma yore son Geo."

The old lady smiled. She had no teeth but her expression was sweet. "Much obliged." She clasped the letter against her breast. "He's coming! He'll hep Hanner."

"Can't I help her?"

The proud head went up and she slipped the letter in her pocket. "No, thankee. Much obliged you coming to visit her. But we're getting along fine." She turned to go back in the house but hesitated, too polite to leave MaryJake alone on the porch.

MaryJake said good-bye and went slowly down the trail. It was clear from what Hannah's grandma said that even though George was away in the penitentiary somebody on the ridge was running his still. Somebody was furnishing the backings to make Hannah drunk. But MaryJake found that she couldn't hold it against him. She wouldn't have Hannah suffer so for anything. The only answer was to get Hannah to a tooth doctor.

FIFTEEN

S HE FOUND MIZ BENNETT working in the
garden. MaryJake had trouble keeping back the tears
as she told her about Hannah. MaryJake knew that a boy
wouldn't cry or talk so much, but her tongue ran away with
her. She finally sealed her lips together to keep from break-
ing down.

"You're too tenderhearted, Jake." Miz Bennett leaned
on her hoe. "Life's hard on folks with a tender heart.
'Specially when they can't do a thing to change what's
happening."

For the rest of the day MaryJake fretted over Hannah.
Almost as unsettling was the short rations the barn in-
habitants were on. They got one meal a day, at night,
mostly nubbins about three inches long with a handful of
hay and a sprinkling of grain.

After chores MaryJake and Miz Bennett ate their own
quick, silent supper.

When the cleaning up was done, MaryJake said, "I'll
take a little walk."

Miz Bennett glanced out the kitchen's only window. "Dark's coming soon. Don't go far, Jake."

MaryJake nodded and struck out for the the graveyard where she lay on the overturned tombstone and cried. When she could straighten up and wipe her face she looked around. A quietness was everywhere here, an old, old quietness that she had noticed before, though usually she was too busy tending to herself to ponder it. Now that the sun had set, the roses willingly scented the warm air with their perfume. The trees at the edge of the clearing did not stir. A bird, trying to make itself safe and comfortable for the night, rustled in the bushes.

MaryJake laid her hand on her favorite inscription. The stone felt dry and crinkly with algae and warm from the day's sun. For the first time she paid attention to whose stone it was: his name was Millard. By squinting she read that he was killed in the Waxahatchie disaster, leaving a wife to mourn him. His wife must have written the poem about how their lives were riven because below it, covered by weeds, was the lament, "Oh, Millard, Millard!" MaryJake could almost hear her crying out. In the quiet she whispered, "Oh, Hannah . . . oh, David . . . Paul . . . Rose . . . Adder. . . . He was an obedient dog. . . . I was an obedient child. . . . Ma, Ma, how could you leave me?"

Dark had crept out of the woods and surrounded her before she stood up to go. She sensed that the peace she felt as she closed the gate must come from knowing other people had hurt too and somehow kept on living. As she approached the cabin she heard the steady sound of Miz Bennett's rocking chair. They sat for a while on the porch without talking before going in to bed.

Hannah did not come down from the ridge for a week. When she rode Buck into Miz Bennett's yard, leading Bennie, she wore her usual faded dress, washed clean. Her face was no longer swollen and her hair was combed, but her eyes looked as if they wanted to shut themselves against the hurtful sunlight. MaryJake tried not to show how glad she was to see her. She wanted to grab Hannah's hand and pat her shoulder and ask how her teeth were. But Hannah only said, "Hidy. Want to go bottle hunting?" She acted as if they'd seen each other the day before.

As they turned Buck's and Bennie's heads toward the woods, MaryJake said, "Let's go my way today," and she took the lead. When Hannah realized that MaryJake's way went through the clearing, she halted Buck and dismounted.

"No, no, Jake. We can't go that way." She had turned white under her freckles.

"Why not? It's shorter."

"There's something bad that way—a hant that'll follow you and pesticate you for the rest o'your life."

"What kind of hant?"

"One that lives high in the trees. A man Uncle George knows was in the graveyard digging for buried treasure— the hant come down and nearly caught him."

"How did it look?"

Hannah spoke earnestly. "It looked like a woman, but that don't mean it was a woman. It come down that tree easy as a monkey, hollering ever' breath like Miz Bennett's peafowl."

"What did it do?"

"He didn't wait to see. He went from there so fast he

left his money needle behind. And his shovel. And his dinner pail."

MaryJake hesitated. She'd spent time in the clearing and knew firsthand that no hants guarded the place. Should she tell Hannah the story was untrue? Finally she said, "Who told you this?"

Hannah was too worried to take offense at MaryJake's doubt. "My uncle George. He knows everything."

"Is the graveyard haunted because of the buried money?"

"An awful thing happened in a house that useter be there, Uncle George said. Somebody murdered a man and his whole family—chirren too. Then they set the house afire. We oughten to even be talking about it." She glanced around and shuddered.

"But—but, if there's buried money somebody would have dug it up, hant or no hant. I know I would've."

Hannah stiffened and her eyes dared MaryJake to dispute her. "Uncle George said it's the truth."

MaryJake pressed her lips together to hold back her words. They remounted and followed Hannah's way through the woods to the highway.

Every time they hunted bottles it seemed to MaryJake they met more and more hitchhikers. Folks were on the move, trying to get someplace else. Mostly they were men, sometimes dressed in suits and carrying rolled up newspapers. A few smiled and spoke but mainly they walked past, their shoulders slumped, their eyes on the ground. Some of them stirred a bad odor in the air as if they hadn't bathed in a long time. Others smelled like smoking tobacco. MaryJake felt glad she had a place in the world to belong.

They hadn't hunted bottles in nearly two weeks. Now they found so many they stayed out till the sun was near setting in a sky redder than Hannah's hair. MaryJake remembered Ma and Pa had said what colored the sky that way was the topsoil of Oklahoma and Texas blowing away. Because of that she had figured out that Pa wouldn't have gone to either of those places. He likely would have gone farther, maybe to California, to the Pacific Ocean. And I'm going there too, soon as I save enough money, she assured herself.

When they hurried back to the spring and dumped their sack, they burst out laughing. "Rich! We're rich!" MaryJake jumped up and down, slapping her hands against her overall legs.

"Fifteen! The most we ever found," Hannah said. She looked serious. "I decided not to buy candy or strawberry ice cream—nothin' like that. I'm going to get my teeth fixed, if I can find somebody to carry me to the tooth doctor."

"I'll add my money in with yours so you can go sooner," MaryJake offered.

The proud look so much like her grandma's came over Hannah's face, her head lifting, her chin jutting forward. "No, thankee. I'll save it quick enough."

SIXTEEN

MOST NIGHTS after Miz Bennett blew out the lamp, MaryJake put her mind to the problem of getting money for Hannah's teeth. Though Hannah brought payment for the bottles on time, the money wasn't enough to pay a tooth doctor. We can pick berries and sell them, MaryJake thought. The green blackberries had already turned red and would soon swell and ripen to a shiny black. She sat up on her shuck mattress trying to keep it from rustling and disturbing Miz Bennett. If people in the settlement wouldn't buy the berries door-to-door she and Hannah could stand with Buck and Bennie out on the highway. Maybe people would stop out of curiosity.

Another thing—at the end of summer, muscadines would ripen in the woods. Everybody liked to eat muscadines. MaryJake hugged her knees as her mind raced away. And when winter came, why not dig sassafras roots? People needed sassafras tea for tonics. They could hunt chinquapins, and surely there were chestnuts left somewhere. Hannah would know. Something else, maybe they could peddle eggs now that the chickens, turkeys, and geese were laying again. The guineas had tapered off with their output or maybe they had another hidden nest.

MaryJake's heart beat faster at the thought of the money piling up, money to fix Hannah's teeth and money to take her westward to find David and Paul. She made such wild plans she had trouble sleeping. What finally calmed her down was the knowledge that first of all she and Hannah had to haul home the animal feed with the help of Buck and Uncle George's cart. Tomorrow. Which meant MaryJake would have to go into the settlement, a place she had vowed never to go.

When Buck pulled the two-wheel cart into Miz Bennett's yard next day, MaryJake looked it over and agreed Uncle George had done a good job. They decided that Hannah should ride in the cart and apply the wooden stick against the wheel to brake the cart on the steep grade going toward the settlement. That would keep the cart from running over Buck. MaryJake was to walk alongside the cart and help the brakes hold it back when needed. Then when the cart stuck in the sand beds, she was to give the back end a heave to help Buck pull it out.

They traveled down the trail quicker than MaryJake expected. Before she was ready they were rolling through the middle of the settlement. MaryJake tried to see it all in one look—several dwelling houses, some not as neat as Miz Bennett's but all of them newer and better built; the school, white and not as large as MaryJake's last school; the store painted orange, a barbershop leaning against the side of it. In the center of everything stood the rock castle, finer than MaryJake had imagined it. The odd-shaped rocks that built it shaded from brown to tan to cream and fitted together in a complicated pattern. A climbing rose twined around the posts of the porch facing the road where MaryJake and Hannah paused with Buck and the cart, looking.

At the left corner of the house stood a rounding turret higher than the second story of the castle. The turret was topped with stone scallops trimmed with tan bricks. What must it be like to stand up there and look away off? How would you get up there? To the right hand of the yard grew a big tree MaryJake couldn't identify, thick with leaves that cast a deep shade over several chairs and a swing. Through the screen of the open front door came a tune played on what MaryJake thought must be a piano.

"They got a bathroom," whispered Hannah.

How did Ma know about this place? Did she come from this house? wondered MaryJake, thinking about how Ma loved music, spoke the language just right, and had proper manners. Was she a servant here? A member of the family?

"Who lives here?" she asked in a low voice.

Before Hannah could say, a loud laughing voice came from behind them. "Hey, Hannah Meow-ry! Your noble steed's run away! Better catch him!"

MaryJake turned to see a boy about their age whack Buck on the hucklebone with his open hand, startling the calf into a run. The boy chased after him, yelling, and whacked him again. Buck lost his head and plunged across the road just as a mile-long car steadily blowing a deep, hoarse foghorn hurtled down the road without lessening its speed. A wide shiny bumper stuck out in front as if it were clearing the way for the grand car, and two big shiny headlamps above the bumper looked like eyes—eyes that saw Buck and meant to do him harm. The terrified calf leaped clear but the car struck the rear end of the cart and knocked off a wheel. A bunch of boys who had been standing around the store door whooped as they joined the boy running after the wheel rolling away down the road. When they caught it, the boy, followed by his friends, rolled it back to the cart where Hannah was patting and talking comfort to Buck, whose sides heaved with his hard breathing.

MaryJake stood in the road, glaring after the car. Through the oil fumes and roiling dust she saw its shining back bumper rolling steadily away from the damage it had done. She turned her attention to the boys larking toward her with the runaway wheel. The main boy was laughing as he ran along rolling the wheel. It was his strong white teeth more than his fine looks that set MaryJake off. Why should he have teeth like that and Hannah have her rotted, hurting teeth? Why did he have the right to hit Buck and make fun of Hannah and break George's cart? Now Miz Bennett's animals would go hungry.

SEVENTEEN

BEFORE THE BOY could lay down the wheel MaryJake was on him like a guinea on a squash bug. She hit him in the face with her doubled up fists. She knew it hurt because her fists were bony and knuckled. She tried to snatch his ear off his head, remembering how bad it hurt when Pa did it to her. She socked his nose with all her might to make blood run down over those white teeth that weren't laughing now. She wanted to knock the teeth out of his mouth to make him snaggle toothed but that hurt her hand. She whammed him on his arms, hoping to break his bones. She kicked him on his legs with her calloused bare feet, on his shinbone where it hurt the most. She felt like a dust devil, fists and feet flying, and she bit her tongue to keep from saying out loud some of Pa's favorite words that burned in her mind.

The boy was so startled he didn't do anything at first. MaryJake had the impression that everybody was dumbstruck except her and she meant to work this boy over good and proper before he came to himself. She knew this rage she was taking out on the boy wasn't only because of what he had done. She knew it was a mixture of Pa and Ma throwing her away, Paul and David being gone, Adder in the fighting pit, and having no money for Hannah's teeth.

The boy was nearly twice as big as MaryJake. When he came to himself, he sent her flying across the road with one sweep of his arm, knocking the breath out of her. She lay sprawled in the ditch, gasping for air. Hannah came to help her up. The boy's friends gathered round him. Buck, still looking befuddled, waited with the tilted one-wheeled cart.

The wide screen door of the rock castle slammed behind the prettiest girl MaryJake ever saw. She was real blond, not cotton-headed like MaryJake would be if she were not walnut brown now. Her golden hair curled about her shoulders, her blue eyes blazed at the boys. Even though she had beautiful white teeth like the boy, MaryJake didn't desire to knock them out because the girl hadn't insulted Buck and Hannah.

"Titus Sylvanus Agnew!" the girl shouted. "I'm going to tell on you! You won't get to go to the picture show either! What did you do?" She looked at the wheel flat on the ground, and then at the cart. She wore a blue dress and white shoes and socks with not a spot of dirt on them. MaryJake suddenly realized that she and Hannah were the only ones here without shoes and socks.

Now a woman came out of the house, and a man crossed the road from the store. The boys, except for Titus Agnew, withdrew to safety but stayed within listening distance.

The Agnew boy wiped his bloody face on his shirt

sleeve. "He don't fight fair," he complained to the man and woman.

"'Doesn't,'" corrected the woman. "What happened?"

Titus Agnew said, "I bet he's a gypsy. He fights like a girl, a low-down trickster."

"Girls fight fair, you dirt clod! I'll show you," and the blond girl drew back her fist.

The woman caught the girl's arm and shook her. "Stop it, Erleen. If there's another fight we'll never straighten things out." The woman turned to the man who had stood the wheel on end and was examining it.

"Hannah," he said, "is Buck all right?" His voice was slow and easy.

Hannah nodded.

"Fine. Now help me see how this wheel fits on and we'll have your wagon fixed in no time. Where're you going?"

"We come for Miz Bennett's critter feed." Hannah's voice trembled.

"Titus, you lift up the wagon bed and hold it."

"Come, Erleen. You must finish your practice before we go." MaryJake watched the girl follow the woman into the house.

The boy's face turned red from holding the weight of the cart for so long. Finally the wheel was shoved on and secured. The man wiped his hands on a white handkerchief from his hip pocket. "Bring the wagon, Hannah. Titus will load the feed for you."

They crossed the road to a side door of the store, the man and the boy leading the way. Hannah walked at Buck's head with a hand on his halter. MaryJake came behind the cart, listening to the instructions the man gave the Agnew boy about placing the feed in the cart to keep the load balanced. She intended to see that he did the loading right. He kept wiping his nose and his lower lip pouted—either it was swollen from MaryJake's blows or he was still angry. Maybe both. MaryJake herself had calmed down, satisfied that she had given this white-toothed boy a just punishment. She bet he'd think twice before he hit Buck again. But she knew she could never have damaged him so much if she hadn't taken him by surprise.

EIGHTEEN

O N   T H E   W A Y   H O M E   both Hannah and
MaryJake walked. Going uphill with a loaded cart
made a difference to Buck. He needed lots of help over
the rocks and through the sinking sand beds. When they
rolled into Miz Bennett's yard she came to meet them,
looking pleased and proud.

"What a fine thing to have enough feed again! I'd
rather my animals—and Jake too, o'course—have food than
me." She smiled at MaryJake. "I'll hep you store it to keep
it safe from the wild critters."

Opening the sacks of feed was fun. Miz Bennett
showed them how to start the string a certain way so
that the stitching would unravel, leaving the string in one
length. "I save string. It comes in handy. When you need
string nothing else will do." She hung it on a nail in the
feed room. By the time they finished, the animals came
trailing in for the night.

Hannah and Buck left with a basket of early "roastnears" and a bunch of "creases"—what Ma called "cress"—

that Miz Bennett had picked from the spring. They parted without mentioning what had happened in the settlement. For one reason, MaryJake didn't want to dim Miz Bennett's pleasure in having a good supply of feed in the barn. For another, she felt she ought to be ashamed of herself, but she wasn't. She might even laugh if she told Miz Bennett, especially if Hannah helped tell the story.

By the time Miz Bennett put the light out, MaryJake was so sore and stiff she could hardly stretch her body flat on the mattress without groaning. What a wallop that boy gave her, but she gave him a few too! She thought of a jeer Pa used to laugh about:

> Fight, fight, you ain't no kin.
> Kill each other, ain't no sin.

She was no kin to him, she was sure of that. But the woman was a different matter. MaryJake didn't want to think about her but she couldn't help it—that woman coming out of the rock castle looked like Ma—a younger, softer-living Ma. And the way she corrected the boy's grammar when he'd just been through a fight—that was exactly like Ma getting after MaryJake.

What would life be like in that house, with a bathroom, a piano, and that pretty girl in the blue dress? Going to the picture show! MaryJake had never seen a picture show. She had barely heard about such a thing. And she had never seen such an elegant monster of a car as the one that aimed to hit Buck. What an amazing and terrible day this had been.

She was beginning to realize that there were many things she needed to find out about. Maybe she should go to school. But then she'd have to buy new overalls and a shirt—one set would do, and Miz Bennett could wash it on Saturdays while MaryJake stayed inside wearing her nightshirt. But she didn't want to spend any of her bottle money for clothes, so maybe she should stay out of school. She could manage that easily. Nobody ever came around checking. It seemed that the schools had more pupils than they could afford already.

NINETEEN

N OW THAT THE GARDEN was well up out of
the ground, the poultry were allowed inside the rail
fence to check the plants for bugs and worms. MaryJake
liked to hear the happy murmur of the guineas and the
hens as they worked from sunrise to sunset. Only once had
she seen the puffing adder; he lay so still in the shade of
the pea vines that not even the sharp-eyed guineas saw
him. She believed the snake lived in the feed room and
feasted on pesky mice because she never found mouse
pills, and no holes were ever gnawed in the sacks of grain.

MaryJake and Hannah worked hard roaming the cutover hillsides picking berries, hunting guinea nests, searching for bottles and jars. To sell their berries, eggs, and what
garden produce Miz Bennett could spare, they parked the
loaded cart beside the highway with Buck and Bennie
standing nearby in the shade. They smoothed a board with
sand and used a chicken feather to letter a sign with poke-
berry ink, a deep purplish red. The sign, alerting drivers
that ahead was a stand, read: VEGS. ETC. CHUFA STOP.

The chufa nuts caused the most interest. City people hadn't heard of them. MaryJake didn't know of a living thing that didn't love chufas, including herself and Hannah. They each kept a pocket full to give them strength for their work. Culver went wild when he smelled chufas.

Hannah said, "Granny says chufas taste sweeter'n chestnuts."

"Better than peanuts!" MaryJake agreed.

They worried because their supply was getting low and the new crop couldn't be dug till fall.

MaryJake thought selling by the roadside was exciting. Between customers she and Hannah brushed Buck and Bennie and polished their hooves with meat grease. They looked very fine, MaryJake thought, fit subjects for a picture, and some people who stopped used their Brownie box cameras to snap them.

Bennie sometimes had to stay home and plow. Hannah no longer went to the post office looking for letters. MaryJake decided George must have gotten a parole as he would probably be the plowman.

By this time Miz Bennett knew that they collected and sold bottles. To Hannah's surprise, Miz Bennett didn't object. "Whiskey can be bad, but you and Jake are going to use the money for good," was all she said.

MaryJake's hoard of money grew, but her overalls and shirt were so faded and worn, she and Miz Bennett finally agreed that new ones had to be bought.

"How much you reckon they'll set me back?" MaryJake worried. Miz Bennett didn't know because she hadn't bought clothes of any kind in forty years.

Nervous as she was about going into the settlement

again, MaryJake accompanied Miz Bennett the next time she went to the post office to collect her Confederate pension check. Afterward they stopped in at the orange-colored store.

The easy-talking man who had put the cart wheel back on was behind the counter. Miz Bennett called him Mr. Agnew. To MaryJake's relief he showed no recognition of her. She hoped he had forgotten about the fight. She had found out from Hannah that Titus Agnew was this man's nephew and the pretty blond girl his daughter. Hannah supposed the woman who came out of the rock house was Mr. Agnew's wife, the mother of the girl, but she didn't know their names. "The woman's a teacher, that I know," Hannah added.

Miz Bennett held up overalls against MaryJake till she found a pair a couple of inches too big. "These'll give you room to grow. And this shirt—you like it all right? Long sleeves will save you from the briars, and this dark color won't show the berry stains." MaryJake had been so used to her white short-sleeved shirt and worn overalls she knew she wouldn't be comfortable in this stiff dark blue pair with the brown shirt. She never wore undergarments and Miz Bennett didn't question her about the matter. In that way Miz Bennett was like Miss Celestine—minding her own business.

MaryJake paid $1.75 and Mr. Agnew handed her the clothes in a paper bag. She was in a hurry to leave while nobody else was in sight, but before they could get out the door the woman who looked like Ma came in. She greeted Miz Bennett, then turned her eyes full on MaryJake. They were exactly like Ma's all-seeing clear green eyes flecked with gold, but this woman wasn't fearful of what she would see looking at you. She held MaryJake's eyes steadily, and MaryJake did not falter until she remembered her own green eyes that were so much like Ma's. She blinked and half turned away.

"Is this your grandson, Miz Bennett?" the woman asked.

Miz Bennett coughed lightly. "This is Jake Smith, Miss Myra. He's staying at my house till his folks send for him."

The green eyes turned on MaryJake again like glowing lights. MaryJake refused to return the look. "Jake Smith? Where are you from, Jake?"

That was something Miz Bennett had never asked her. MaryJake didn't think this woman should ask it either. "Other side of the mountain, ma'am," she said watching a car pull in to the gas pump.

"Oh? You'll be coming to school, won't you?" Miss Myra smoothed her light hair back from her face. MaryJake stared at the diamond ring on her slender white hand. Big as a dime it was, and more dazzling than her green eyes. A clutch of prongs standing out from the gold band held the diamond so it could be seen from all angles.

MaryJake forgot she'd been asked a question till she heard Miz Bennett answering for her. "He might can." Miz Bennett hefted her sack. "It's hot today. We'd best get on up the hill."

On the way home, MaryJake noticed how quick and short the old woman's breaths came, almost like little pants. Miz Bennett shifted the paper bag to first one hip then the other and her feet seemed heavy. At the next log they came to, MaryJake set down her sacks. "Let's take a little rest."

After they had settled themselves and caught their breaths, MaryJake asked, "Where does the teacher live?"

"In the rock castle. A passel of 'em live in there. The storekeeper, Mr. Agnew—a real truepenny. The teacher, Miss Myra. Their chile—name of Erleen. The storekeeper's nephew, Titus." Miz Bennet sighed. "He come from away somewheres after his folks got carried off by the flu. They all rich."

"How did they get rich?"

Miz Bennett thought for a moment. "Well, Miss Myra was a Kirkbank. Her folks owned all the land from here to the river. They sold timber. They mined coal. They growed cotton. Whatever they did turned into money."

"Anybody else in that family?" MaryJake pressed her.

"The varmint, but he's got his own place down on the creek. The castle's big enough to hold scores o'folks. Miss Myra's sister—she useter live there."

Ma? Could it be? MaryJake held her breath, waiting.

Miz Bennett stood up, ending their conversation. MaryJake knew the old lady couldn't walk uphill and talk at the same time, but she couldn't resist asking, "What was her sister's name?"

"I fergit." Miz Bennett worked her jaws as if she were chewing her cud. "She went off somewheres. Took a baby chile with her that belonged to her sister—her sister that died."

She's too tired, MaryJake thought. I'll ask her more questions another time, maybe tonight on the porch.

TWENTY

B UT THAT WASN'T to be. As they were finishing
supper they heard a jaunty ringing of a bell in the
front yard, and MaryJake knew she was as good as found
out. Miss Celestine and ole Dink. Of all places, why had
they come here?

MaryJake stayed in the corner that was the kitchen,
putting things away while Miz Bennett went to the porch
to make the guest welcome. MaryJake could hear the glad
lilt of Miss Celestine's voice as she explained her and Dink's
needs for the night. Then Miz Bennett called, "Jake! Come
help Miss Celestine!" and MaryJake, with dragging steps,
went.

Miss Celestine turned to look at her when she stepped
through the door, but MaryJake kept to the shadows and
bent her head. Miz Bennett, proud as always, pulled her
forward. "This here is Jake Smith. He's staying a bit with
me, and he's the handiest thing alive with animals. He'll
fix up your horse."

Miss Celestine's expression gave away nothing, but

for the first time MaryJake ever remembered, her flow of words dried up. After the silence she said in her bright way, "I'll thank you, Jake, to take care of ole Dink. Don't let him over drink with the water."

"Yessum," MaryJake muttered, escaping down the steps. Dink was as big and bony as ever. MaryJake led him to a stump, which she stood on, and began unloading him. The two women took the bags and sacks as MaryJake brought them to the porch and stacked them against the wall. They chatted like old friends, sweeping the porch before laying the pallet. Miss Celestine showed off the quilts as they spread them on the floor, and then Miz Bennett took her inside to show off the Rainbow Falls quilt she had made.

While MaryJake oversaw Dink rolling in the sand, she was remembering the last time this happened in exactly the same way, and the old ache came back in her chest. Then it was Pa seeing to Dink, and she was helping Miss Celestine make the pallet.

She led Dink to the spring to drink from the stream. With her eyes she carefully measured the water he sucked in, for it was just-out-of-the-ground cold and Dink was sweating from his long day. She stopped him before he had his fill, and took him back to the house in the twilight. Inside the barnyard fence she set him out a half bucket of sweet feed and some hay. Tomorrow she would find tender grass for his old teeth to chew. He sighed and rubbed his head against her shoulder before he began eating. None of the animals awakened except Culver in his pen by the barn door. He raised his head and grunted a question, then snuggled down in the straw again.

The lamp was lit on the kitchen table and Miss

Celestine was unwrapping the goody feast while Miz Bennett sat watching with shining eyes. MaryJake sat down too, remembering Paul and David's intent eyes that other time. Bananas again! And square chocolate-covered cookies. Miss Celestine smiled at MaryJake. "Jennie Wrenns—or is it Jennie Lynns? I forget. But they're good. Take two. And then look at this homemade salt-rising bread—that wild yeast makes it smell like rotten cabbage, but it tastes like manna. The Widow Thornton over at Six Mile made it. Here's butter in this jar, melted from the heat of the day. It'll spread just fine."

What a delicious goody feast! MaryJake knew how ole Dink felt eating his sweet feed and hay tonight. After the cleanup, they blew out the lamp and went to the porch, and there Miss Celestine told the story of her quest. MaryJake wondered how many thousand times she had told it in these three years. Miz Bennett sat in her rocker without moving, entranced as Ma used to be. MaryJake was entranced too as she listened to Miss Celestine arguing with the Lord.

At the end Miss Celestine said softly, "I admit, I'm getting tired. And Dink is 'most too old to travel. But I know the Lord will look after us until His purpose is accomplished."

"Amen," breathed Miz Bennett.

"When I feel down low, dragging bottom, I think of the lost and unwanted boys who'll have a home when I do find the right place. That keeps me going. Just last month, over in Mississippi—Okolona, I think it was—I stayed at a place where there were two little boys—towheads, five and six years old. Their uncle is tired of bothering with them. It's boys like that the Lord told me to take in. 'Don't turn any away,' he instructed me. And I won't."

MaryJake heard her heart knocking against her ribs as she leaned forward and whispered, "By what names were those boys called?"

"Nobody called their names, and the boys didn't talk." Miss Celestine inclined her head in the shadows. "Their uncle's name is Wildsmith."

Pa's brother who was too sorry to eat pie! How could Ma and Pa have left her brothers there? MaryJake thought of the money she had saved toward her westward trip. Miss Celestine's words had suddenly given her a more definite goal to aim for. She could go for her brothers on the bus and bring them here. Somehow she must make more money to help Miz Bennett feed everybody.

A shed room would have to be built onto the house for the boys. That would take more and more money. If she could hire George, who was a good builder, maybe he'd stay out of trouble and then Hannah would be glad. Her plans ran away with her till she had to stand up to keep from exploding.

Miss Celestine's night prayer was thankfulness for her safe journey and for those who were willing to take her in each night. She prayed for all the homeless in the world, especially the boys. Then she reminded God of His promise to show her the place for His building project, and she ended with "Praise the Lord!"

In the dark, MaryJake washed her face, hands, and feet in the pan at the shelf, then tiptoed inside. Miz Bennett had already pulled the mattress from under the bed and spread it with the Rainbow Falls quilt. MaryJake felt Miz

Bennett glancing at her uneasily, which made her want to say something but she couldn't think what. As Miz Bennett knelt to say her prayers, MaryJake stood beside the bed to help her up. Still holding the old woman's hand, MaryJake whispered, "Much obliged for being so good to me." Tears came in Miz Bennett's eyes. She patted MaryJake before blowing out the lamp.

In the dark, MaryJake undressed and put on Mr. Bennett's nightshirt. She knew as plain as day that Miss Celestine recognized her. But she also knew Miss Celestine would be true to her honor code not to meddle in anybody else's life unless she was asked. Still, MaryJake realized the time was soon coming when she would have to confess. What would Hannah think?

TWENTY·ONE

MISS CELESTINE lingered at Miz Bennett's, explaining that Dink needed a rest. She insisted on taking Miz Bennett's place helping MaryJake with chores, giving Miz Bennett the excuse that ole Dink required a lot of care. Between chores she walked everywhere, as if she were hunting guinea nests, looking and thinking. One day MaryJake and Hannah, riding the calves, found her standing on the rock that jutted over the hollow. She stared at the make-believe berry pickers, but asked no questions. Another time she came walking out of the woods on MaryJake's path from the clearing. MaryJake wished she knew what was in her mind.

MaryJake noticed Hannah acting droopy but she didn't know how to find out what was bothering her. Late one afternoon as they washed bottles at the spring she heard Hannah sucking air through her teeth.

"Is the ache coming back?" MaryJake asked.

"It does that, seems like," Hannah said, stopping the

sound and putting a light lift in her voice that warned she didn't want pity.

MaryJake stood up. "Don't be so puffed up," she snarled. "We're friends, Hannah Mowry. We're supposed to help each other." She softened at the look of dread in Hannah's eyes. "You think you're in for a bad spell?"

Hannah stopped sloshing sand and water in a bottle. "Yeah," she said in a smothered voice. "The pain starts out 'bout this long"—she measured an inch between a finger and thumb—"and comes only once in a while. Then it grows this long"—she measured twelve inches between her hands—"and comes all the time till I just can't stand it—till I'd rather die than have another one. And what Granny does for me is kinda like dying. 'Cept I feel so terrible sick when I wake up. And Uncle George gets madder'n a hornet."

"We've got to get you to the tooth doctor. I'll leave you borrow what money I've saved." Hannah made a move to object but MaryJake stopped her. "You can pay me back before I need it."

They worked in silence a while. Then MaryJake said, "I don't see any other way but to tell Miss Celestine. She'll know what to do. She'll pray about it—funny the talking she does with God—but, Hannah, she won't tell anybody else but God."

MaryJake knew the thought of the awful pain Hannah faced had humbled her. She hardly protested at all, and by the time they loaded the sack of bottles on Bennie and she mounted Buck, Hannah had agreed MaryJake could talk with Miss Celestine about a tooth doctor.

"Your grandma will have to know," MaryJake said,

walking alongside Hannah and the calves a short way up the ridge path. "And Miz Bennett too. But nobody else." Hannah nodded, nudged Buck with her heels, and clucked her tongue at Bennie.

MaryJake felt jumpy that night after supper, sitting on the porch step with Miz Bennett and Miss Celestine in the dark behind her. Miss Celestine had just said she wondered if God was communicating with her. "Since I rode ole Dink into your yard, a different sort of feeling has settled over me, almost like I'm in a dream. I've never felt this way before and I can't help thinking I'd better prepare myself for a happening. Can it be Dink's going to die on me? Is God getting me ready for an event?"

Neither MaryJake nor Miz Bennett answered. MaryJake knew Miz Bennett was as unknowing as she was.

"The Lord knows I'm tired," Miss Celestine continued. "And so is ole Dink. We're both just about wore out. I'm yearning for this to be the chosen place—I've tramped all over these hills inviting God to show me that this is the place—but no sign comes."

MaryJake had never heard Miss Celestine sound so discouraged. It brought to mind her own discouragement over Hannah. She said in the silence, "Hannah's fixing to get sick again." Miz Bennett stopped rocking.

Miss Celestine said, "How is that?"

MaryJake said slowly, wanting to choose the right words to make Miss Celestine understand, "You've noticed how decayed her front teeth are? The top ones, not the bottom ones. And some of her back teeth. When the pain comes on her so bad, her grandma makes her drink the backings from the still. It puts Hannah in a stupor, like a dead person, only stinking and filthy and . . . and . . ." MaryJake shuddered to remember. "Uncle George is fearful Hannah will get poisoned, or come to depend on it all the time—a drunk. Hannah says he's a dreadnought when he's in a temper. He just got out of prison for moonshining. Hannah's grandma is like a little sick monkey, and she's blind. Hannah's scared he'll hurt her." MaryJake stood up, held on to a porch post, and faced Miss Celestine and Miz Bennett, though she couldn't see them. "Hannah *must* go to the tooth doctor. She—she's going to die, I'm thinking. And we've saved money from the bottles and from peddling the berries and everything. Reckon you can talk to God about Hannah?"

Miss Celestine didn't hesitate. "Of course. Right now." And MaryJake heard the rustling of her skirts as she knelt by her chair. MaryJake dropped to her knees beside Miz Bennett's rocker. She felt Miz Bennett's hand rest on top of her bowed head.

They prayed for Hannah for half an hour or more, with Miss Celestine sounding like she addressed a poem to God. She prayed about Hannah's home and her grandma and her uncle. She asked God to open up a way for Hannah to go to a dentist, a good dentist who would be willing to help her for the price she could afford to pay. In her grand voice she made detours now and then to explore the strange feeling that had come over her lately, asking that she should have a clear insight into what God wanted of her. She prayed for homeless boys everywhere, especially the two little towheads in Okolona, Mississippi.

MaryJake felt the tears splashing on her hands. Could God possibly care about Paul and David? If He cared about Hannah and her pain, she knew He cared about her little brothers. But now her money for fetching the boys was promised for repairing Hannah's teeth. When would she ever see Paul and David again?

Her knees began hurting on the hard floor, taking her mind off of her crying. She shifted her weight backward onto her heels. Miss Celestine came to what Ma called the epilogue, the summing up. She praised God for the starry canopy of heaven, for pure water to drink from the bowels of the earth, for a place of refuge tonight, and for His continuing mercy to them all, amen.

Without speaking they went to bed, MaryJake holding Miz Bennett's elbow to steady her through the familiar dark.

TWENTY-TWO

F OR SEVERAL DAYS MaryJake and Miss Celestine
walked up to the ridge to plan with Hannah and
her grandma. They counted over the money MaryJake
and Hannah had made from the bottles and from peddling. The sum of it came to $51.11. Miss Celestine found
out from the post office lady the time the bus passed by
on the highway going to town and what the fare would
be—50¢ one way. Hannah had never been to town. She
couldn't go by herself. Miss Celestine, the only one with
any know-how about the outside world, would have to
go with her. That meant $2 every round trip for them.
Mr. Agnew wrote on a paper the name and address of
their family dentist, who charged $1 a visit, and gave it
to Miss Celestine. Since Hannah didn't have fifty teeth
in her mouth, they figured that after the work was finished and the bus tickets paid for, they might even have
money left over. MaryJake admired Miss Celestine's man-
aging ways.

"Hannah needs a dress and shoes," Miss Celestine said

during chores one day. "She can't go to town ragged and barefooted. I don't know how to solve that, Jake."

MaryJake didn't hesitate. "I do. Give me a little time."

When Miz Bennett went to the garden to pick vegetables, MaryJake pulled out the quilt drawer and opened her bundle. She found the green dress with white leaves tumbling down the front and shook it out. It had been too big for her the one time she wore it. It ought to be a good fit for Hannah, she thought. How glad she was she had folded it carefully when she put it away that day at the dye pot. When she took out the white bloomers she noticed Ma's handkerchief, with the lump in the corner, which she had forgotten about.

MaryJake stood still, holding her breath, hearing again Ma's instructions: *Tell them your name. . . . Give them this.* She picked up the lace-trimmed square, feeling the weight of whatever was tied in the corner, about the size of a two-bit piece. She laid the handkerchief on the dresser and untied it. What was inside wasn't a quarter but a ring, a gold band with prongs sticking out clasping a diamond the size of a dime. MaryJake bent over, staring hard at it. The ring was a twin to the one on Miss Myra's slim white finger!

MaryJake didn't touch it. Her heart pounding, she hastily retied the handkerchief, stuck it back in the bundle, and shoved the drawer shut. She refolded the dress and bloomers and took them to the porch to lay on top of Miss Celestine's belongings. Then she started along her trail to the clearing. Not only did she need to think but also to find the shoes she had tossed into the bushes last May. After comparing their bare feet in her mind's eye, MaryJake had decided the shoes that blistered her own feet might be just right for Hannah's narrow feet. If the weather hadn't dam-aged them, Hannah would go to town looking proper.

Before entering the graveyard to do her thinking, she searched the bushes for the shoes. She had to find them for Hannah, but they didn't seem to be there. She studied and studied over where she had thrown them, but all she could remember was how glad she was to be rid of them. She hadn't suspected then that someday she would have a friend who needed shoes.

If she retraced her actions of that day she might be reminded of something that would help. She went over to the huge hollow stump of the black walnut tree and looked in. She saw no gleam of dark water, but only dry straw half filling the stump. What an odd thing—she had never seen straw anywhere near the clearing. She reached in and parted the straw to see how deep it was. Underneath she found jars of clear liquid with what looked like bubbles on top—white lightning, she knew, from George's still. She recognized the bottles as the ones she and Hannah had picked up on the road. So this is where he stores it for pickup, she thought. She had never seen any car tracks or footprints in the clearing, but George would be careful to erase those to keep the law from tracking them. She rearranged the straw the way it had been and slowly went through the iron gate to sit on the overturned tombstone.

Her dye pot was the hiding place for George Mowry's whiskey. It was a secure place, keeping the whiskey well away from his cabin, convenient to the highway, and in a haunted clearing that nobody visited out of fear, MaryJake figured, from the tales George spread around. The hiding place hadn't been in use when she first came to Miz

Bennett's because George was off in the penitentiary. What a good thing for me, MaryJake thought. Now she didn't need the stump because the sun daily toasted her a little darker while bleaching her hair a little lighter, and nobody seemed to wonder about it.

But MaryJake realized that the clearing no longer belonged to her. She wouldn't be safe coming here anymore. What about Miss Celestine? What if she happened upon George transacting business? She would be in danger. But Miss Celestine had God on her side.

As MaryJake sat among the gravestones staring at Millard's poem, she decided to look again for where she thought she had thrown the shoes. But this time instead of standing up to search down on the ground, she lay down on the ground and searched up. Sure enough, from flat on her back looking up she saw first one, then the other of the shoes caught in the bushes and kept dry off the ground. They looked as good as they did when MaryJake threw them away. The little stiffness in the leather would soon ease up as Hannah walked in them. MaryJake stuffed the shoes in the bib of her overalls and slowly walked home, thinking about the diamond ring like Myra Kirkbank's that was tied in the corner of Ma's handkerchief, and of George's moonshine hidden in the black walnut stump.

TWENTY-THREE

O N THE DAY of the first visit to the dentist, Hannah came early to Miz Bennett's, her eyes shining with excitement and fright. MaryJake was pleased to see how tamed down Hannah looked with her hair pinned close to her head and the green dress fitting her well enough. Not being used to wearing shoes, she walked in an awkward way and Miss Celestine feared her feet would blister.

"We'll have to walk several blocks," she said, rummaging in one of her sacks. "Maybe you'd better wear these." She pulled out a pair of cotton stockings. Miz Bennett searched the drawers of her pedal sewing machine and found enough elastic to make two garters for holding the stockings up on Hannah's legs.

Miss Celestine wore white, a big change from her dark everyday print dress. At her throat she had pinned a cameo to hold a ruffle of lace, and in each ear gleamed a pearl ear button. She had brushed her black hair upward and pinned the coil on top of her head, then fitted a little white hat over it. The two of them looked exceptionally fine to MaryJake and Miz Bennett, who were standing in the yard, watching as they took Hannah's trail through the woods to the highway. Hannah and Miss Celestine would have to wait by the side of the road till they saw the bus coming, then flag it down.

Suddenly MaryJake's heart gnawed with envy, wishing she could do what they were going to do today and see what they were going to see. That feeling didn't last long though. As she and Miz Bennett turned to each other and smiled, a great hope for Hannah's teeth filled MaryJake with gladness. She hoisted up Culver, who was worrying around at her heels, and took him on the porch to rock him a while. Culver loved to be rocked, especially if MaryJake sang to him. Miz Bennett liked to hear her sing too. While she listened, she picked old blossoms off the petunias and looked for worms and bugs, which she tossed to the chickens. Occasionally she glanced at MaryJake and Culver in the rocking chair and smiled. Her expression said, "You are a funny kind of boy, but I wouldn't change you for a peck of silver dollars," but she didn't say a word.

MaryJake sang old songs she had heard Ma sing, the one Hannah knew about King George's son William, who wore the star on his breast, and another one about kneeling before your lover and measuring how much you loved him by the span of your arms. These two songs had happy words, but MaryJake usually ended a singing session with Miz Bennett's favorite ballad, "Barbrie Allen," the sad story of two lovers who pined away and died. Culver seemed to like that one best of all too. In the parts where she couldn't remember the words MaryJake hummed. She ended the singing story as she recalled it, making her voice exaggerate the words:

> Out o'his grave there grew a red rose, and out o'hers
> a briar.
> They climbed and they climbed the old church tow'r
> Till they could climb no high'r.
> Then they twined and they twined in a true love knot
> The red rose and the briar.

Miz Bennett sighed with satisfaction that the lovers had been reunited after death in that way, and Culver fluttered his eyelids and made a little sound that commanded more. But MaryJake set him down on his four pink hooves saying, "Sooey, sooey! We've got to get busy."

Though she and Miz Bennett worked at many jobs—sunning the quilts on the clothesline, sweeping the floor, bringing water, shelling peas, and anything else they found to do—their talk skipped between home and town, wondering how Hannah and Miss Celestine were getting along.

They sat up late watching the woods for first sight of Miss Celestine's white dress, but nobody came. They finally went inside to an uneasy sleep. All next day they watched more anxiously, but again in vain. It was long after sunset when Hannah and Miss Celestine came walking out of the woods. MaryJake and Miz Bennett saw them coming in the starshine. They met at the edge of the yard near the moonflower vine. Its plate-size white blossoms were unfolding to the night, the sweet perfume drawing insects as big as hummingbirds. The four of them stood together with so much to ask and so much to say they didn't know where to begin. Finally Miss Celestine said, "It's not as bad as we feared. The dentist thinks he can save her teeth, and he's started working on them already."

"He only hurt me a little, not bad like the toothache, and we go back next week and he'll fix some more and we spent the night with some people from a church the dentist knows, and we ate white rolls and roast beef and jello and Miss Celestine says I done good!" MaryJake had never heard Hannah say so many words in one breath.

They fell silent, smiling at each other—a moment that MaryJake never forgot. With no warning the sky above their heads exploded, lighting the world with a brilliant green that revealed everything clearer than daytime, each detail of the vine and the white flowers, of the lace and cameo at Miss Celestine's throat, of the frozen look on her face; of Hannah, her mouth swollen, her red hair escaped from its pins in a wild tangle, her eyes bulging. The deafening roar lasted on and on, echoing, then fading, but the green light continued to illuminate the world while the air sizzled and crackled overhead. MaryJake looked up to see a trail of smoke across the sky. She felt as if she'd been struck by lightning. Miz Bennett covered her eyes with her hands. Hannah kept gasping like a runner caught in a bad dream. Miss Celestine dropped to her knees, her white dress spreading around her, and cried out, "I've been waiting to hear from you, mighty Lord! Wow!"

MaryJake and Hannah huddled with Miz Bennett in a daze. Miss Celestine arose from her knees. "What a marvel we've witnessed! Who has ever been privileged to see such a happening?"

"What was it?" MaryJake whispered, still trembling and half blind.

"The world's coming to an end," Hannah lamented. "And me just now getting my teeth fixed."

Miz Bennett stood as still as a graveyard statue.

"It's all right," Miss Celestine said, the old lilt back in her voice. "We're still all in one piece." She paused to sniff. "Smell that burning? That sulphur odor? Maybe the creation of the world was something like this."

MaryJake's nose felt scalded by the fumes. She coughed. Now that she was recovering a little from her fright she wished God would communicate privately with Miss Celestine and let the rest of them alone. She couldn't stand many such happenings.

Miss Celestine said briskly, "After that blast, Hannah's grandma will think something terrible's happened to her. We'd better head up to the ridge."

MaryJake picked up a package Hannah had dropped. Hannah looked at it as if she'd never seen it before, then remembrance came. "Ohhh, it's a play-pretty for my grandma," she said, reaching for it. "A tune-playing box you wind up. From the dime store." Everyone seemed relieved to bring their attention down to earth, to Hannah's description of the wonders of the dime store. "You can buy anything there you ever thought of," she said, and as they climbed the ridge trail, she sang the notes of the tune her grandma's music box played.

Midway up MaryJake decided she should wait with Miz Bennett on a resting log till Miss Celestine returned. Miz Bennett seemed more short-winded and unsteady than normal. Waiting and listening, MaryJake thought she had never known the world to lie so dark and silent. How easily she could have convinced herself that she had imagined the shattering event of a few minutes ago. But three others had seen and heard it too. MaryJake's ears still felt as if her head was stuffed with cotton. She marveled that nothing appeared changed, though Miss Celestine thought she'd had a message from God.

TWENTY-FOUR

HANNAH WAS FASCINATED by the weekly
trips to town with Miss Celestine. She reported
in detail to MaryJake how the dentist went about his
work, filling her front teeth first—"for cosmetic reasons,"
Hannah quoted him—using a white material that Hannah
called "stuff."

"The white stuff costs more," Hannah reported, her
eyes big and round. "About four dollars for *each* tooth. But
my back teeth, my *molars*, they're gonna be filled with *silver*,
he said."

"Silver mixed with some other things," Miss Celestine
added.

"When he's grinding on my teeth, it does hurt—something awful sometimes—but it never lasts long the way the
toothache did." Hannah made a face, remembering.

What with bus fare for two and tooth repair and medi-
cine to deaden the hurting on the unfilled teeth, their
savings were fast disappearing. MaryJake and Hannah
agreed they had to hunt harder and go farther to find more

bottles. They rode Bennie and Buck through the woods on Hannah's familiar trail. The calves moved at a brisk pace along the shady path. Buck, in the lead, suddenly stiffened his legs and stalled.

"Come on, now, giddyup." Hannah nudged him firmly with her bare feet. He refused to budge, blocking the narrow trail. MaryJake dismounted and gave him a shove from behind with both hands. His hooves were so firmly planted he didn't move. MaryJake put her shoulder to his rear and pushed. Buck pushed back with the power of all four feet. He let out a loud bawl that made MaryJake slacken her push, which released Buck's weight, and he floundered backward. She dodged out of the way.

Hannah dismounted, peering forward in the shadows. "It's not a snake."

"Maybe it's somebody," MaryJake said. "Remember how he acted when he saw me the first time."

"Hold his rope a minute." Hannah walked ahead and bent over. "It's just an ugly ole rock laying here. 'Bout half as big as a syrup bucket. Nothin' to be afraid of, you silly." She grunted as she lifted it and heaved it down in the gulley. She remounted, clucked to Buck, and he went ahead willingly.

MaryJake laughed as she and Bennie followed. "Wonder what he thought it was—a terrapin?"

Upon reaching the highway, they right away found two Mason fruit jars with lids.

"Uncle George'll give top price for these," Hannah said, placing them carefully in the tow sack.

"The start of a lucky day," MaryJake said, scanning each road shoulder as she swung along on Bennie. A car drove slowly past them. Down the road a ways it made a U-turn and came back. MaryJake and Hannah were instantly alert as the car pulled off the highway close to them. Was this their good luck continuing? They watched a young man approach, wondering whether he had picture taking in mind—and maybe a quarter for them to share—or perhaps needed directions.

"Looks like one o'them university fellows," Hannah whispered.

MaryJake examined him, noting his short hair, clean-shaven face, and friendly smile.

"Do you live around here?" he asked.

Hannah nodded and smiled back at him. She liked to show her even white teeth, which MaryJake admitted transformed her from the Hannah she used to be.

"You're riding fine mounts. May I pat them?" He complimented each calf and asked Hannah their names, while MaryJake kept silent, trying to figure him out.

"Say," he said. "Did something strange happen here about a month ago? A real loud noise and a bright light—something like that?"

Now MaryJake joined in. She was curious to know how this fellow would explain God speaking to Miss Celestine. "Yes, near about bedtime—we were in Miz Bennett's front yard—"

"We saw ever' bit of it," Hannah interrupted, showing her teeth again.

The man hesitated, as if he didn't know what he should say next. "I saw it too, but not as close as you, I think. My hobby's astronomy—you know, I study what happens in the sky." He cleared his throat. "I think—I believe—that was a meteorite. I've been searching all over the county since it happened. From what I can judge—as large as it seemed to be—the meteorite could have come through the atmosphere without burning up. It may have landed around here somewhere. Have you noticed anything strange?"

"Noooo," they said, staring at him.

"Probably hit the ground so hard it dug in so you couldn't see it. But there'd be dirt burred up around the hole to show you where it is."

MaryJake and Hannah shook their heads.

"If you find it, will you write me? Here's my address. I'll pay you."

MaryJake slid his card into her overall pocket.

The man looked solemn. "Don't forget now. I'll buy it. Where do you live?"

Hannah turned away, showing she didn't want him coming to her house.

MaryJake said, "At Miz Bennett's." She pointed. "Go past the clearing."

The man thanked them and walked back to his car. Before getting in, he waved.

"Let's find it!" Hannah whispered. "He'll pay!"

"Money!" MaryJake whispered back. "Let's go everywhere—look in mole holes, and fox holes, and tumblebug holes, and woodchuck holes—dig 'em all up!"

"We'll need a shovel—two, so we can both dig. Boy hidy! Lucky day is right."

They continued their patrol of the highway, collecting a few more bottles but watching for spewed-up dirt around a hole as they went along. When the sun showed midday, they took Hannah's trail for Miz Bennett's and the spring. Buck and Bennie, tired and sweating, hurried along through the woods without a balk, knowing that a handful of oats waited for them at home.

TWENTY-FIVE

T HEY RUSHED through washing their day's collection and loaded the sack on Bennie.

"I'll come back after dinner and bring a shovel," Hannah said.

"I'll be ready with our shovel."

Hannah giggled and imitated the town fellow. "Our 'fine mounts' can rest this evening, how about."

MaryJake agreed. "Hunting a meteorite'll be more fun than hunting bottles, but harder, I'll bet."

They roamed the woods all afternoon and all the next day. They did not go beyond George's berry-picking family, but they covered ground MaryJake had never seen before. On the third day they searched along Yellow Bird Creek, a muddy stream choked with branches and struggling its way between hills clear-cut of timber.

MaryJake couldn't believe the barren ugliness she saw on every side. She shut her eyes against it. A creek, she thought, shouldn't look like this. A creek was supposed to run clear and lively through shady woods with wildflowers on the banks.

"Who did this?" she demanded.

"The Kirkbanks that lived in the rock castle—not the ones there now, but their kinfolks. They owned all this land. I reckon they still do, but it's washing away ever'time a rain comes."

"Did the yellow birds leave because the trees were cut?" MaryJake asked, remembering Miz Bennett's quilt.

"I dunno. I can't remember none of them, but my granny does. She says they looked like little parrots. When folks shot into a flock, the hit birds hollered real pitiful. The birds that had got away come back to help and got shot too."

"You know where the waterfall is—Rainbow Falls?"

"I'll show you where it useter to be," Hannah said. "They tore it up hauling the timber out."

What Hannah showed MaryJake looked nothing like a waterfall. It was only muddy water moving along over a few rocks. They kept walking, looking far and near for a hole and a heap of earth. Their shovels were heavy and useless. They decided to leave them under a crooked beech tree growing beside the creek and continued toward the headwaters.

MaryJake had never seen the beginning of a creek. She gazed in amazement at the twin springs that were the source of Yellow Bird Creek. Water boiled up out of the ground like in a great cauldron with a bonfire under it. Around the springs right to the edge grew trees the way they should in a forest. MaryJake looked down the creek, down the path they had come, at the decaying tree stumps, the muddy water, and washed-out gulleys, then looked at the forest around the springs and at the water beginning its journey, clear and cold.

Hannah made a sweeping motion with her arm. "All this green part belongs to Poe Blanton, that moon-eyed boy. He's the varmint, Uncle George says." She lowered her voice to a whisper. "Uncle George saw him once—he's all white, and white haired. He can't see diddle in daylight. If he gets in the sun he'll melt or something."

MaryJake wondered how a person who protected the forest from destruction could be a thief too. The two things didn't seem to go together. "Where is his house?"

"Hereabouts someplace. Want we should try to find him? We're safe to trespass while we're in daylight—he won't be outside."

MaryJake agreed, and they walked into the bird-singing woods, a different world from the one they had left behind. Ferns and late summer flowers and moss like MaryJake hadn't seen in a long time grew under the trees and among the rocks. Red, orange, and brown mushrooms, with an occasional blue one, colored the deep shade. The air smelled cool and green. In a sheltered dell they came upon a cabin smaller than Miz Bennett's but with a porch like hers and covered with such a jumble of flowering plants and vines it was nearly hidden. The window shutters were latched shut, making the house look asleep. MaryJake had never seen a prettier sight.

She went closer, though Hannah warned her back. She couldn't help herself. The flowers against the house and in odd containers on the porch and bedded against the well were all wild. Whoever lived in this house loved wildflowers and had the green thumb to grow them. Standing still in the afternoon warmth, MaryJake smelled the perfumes drifting around her, making her feel light-headed. She breathed deep and deeper. She thought of heaven's incense, of nepenthe, which Ma had told her about. To forget all sorrow, all grief, seemed possible at this moment. She felt she could stay here in this yard forever.

Hannah tugged her arm and hissed a warning. Reluctantly MaryJake let herself be pulled back into the shadows of the forest. She took a last look over her shoulder before they retraced their steps away from the headwaters, past the crooked beech tree where they picked up their shovels, and on homeward, searching, till the last, for a hole surrounded by spewed-up dirt. They did not find it. As they parted at Miz Bennett's spring, tired and discouraged, they agreed to give up the search for the meteorite.

"It's not here. We would've found it," Hannah said.

"I keep thinking there's something we're overlooking. What could it be?" MaryJake watched the sun, ready to drop behind the trees. "Something about Bennie? No—Buck! The day Buck bawled and wouldn't go ahead on the path. That rock! What was that rock like?"

Hannah tried to remember, her eyes unfocused in thought. "Heavy. Black, like soot from the stove."

"Strange?"

"Way yonder strange. But that couldn't be it. It was lying on top of the ground—no hole, no burred-up dirt."

"I don't care—he said did we notice anything strange. And that's the only strange thing in the whole countryside. Even Buck knew it was strange. First thing tomorrow, we'll go get it."

Doubt faded from Hannah's face. She grinned. "Before sunup. I'll wait here at the spring."

"Wish we could go now. But it's too late." All the way to the barn MaryJake chanted, "Go, night! Come, morning! Hurry, hurry!"

The animals saw her coming. Each began his hunger cry, making MaryJake smile, remembering the first night she came here. She picked up the whining Culver and petted and scratched him on the way to his pen. He was peevish because she had stayed away from home so long looking for the meteorite.

"After tomorrow!" she promised, giving him a squeeze before setting him down in his pen. She patted the animals and called them by name as she doled out the food. She slipped Dink's halter on and led him downhill to the stream for a drink. His joints had swollen from rheumatism, making his walk seem painful.

"Good ole horse," she whispered in his ear. "You'll last as long as Miss Celestine needs you."

The lamp was lit in the kitchen corner and the food spread on the table when she came in. The three of them never talked much at supper, mostly because they were tired from the day's work. Tonight MaryJake couldn't have talked anyway; she was too excited. The more she thought of it, the more certain she was that Buck had already found the meteorite. All she and Hannah had to do was refind it tomorrow.

TWENTY-SIX

A S WELL AS MARYJAKE and Hannah knew the trail, they could not agree on the spot where Buck had found the rock. It seemed to take them forever and a day to locate the place. Then on hands and knees they searched the brush inch by inch, raking the leaves with their hands.

"I want to feel that rock," MaryJake said. "I want to know what a meteorite feels like."

Hannah stopped scrabbling in the leaves and stood up. "Now I recollect—after I chunked that rock, I heerd a thump! Like it hit something—maybe a tree, and then I heerd it rolling." That's how they found the unusual black rock: by looking at the base of the larger trees on the side of the trail. MaryJake leaped on the rock and hefted it with two hands. "Bout as big as a sweet potato but a whole lot heavier," she marveled.

On the way back to the cabin, they planned the post-card they would write to the town man. For the first time ever, Hannah ate at Miz Bennett's. In the excitement, she forgot her shyness about table manners. The rock held a place of honor in the center of the table.

Miz Bennett was so awestruck she refused to touch it. "Kinda sacred," she said. "Dropping out o'heaven that way."

Miss Celestine looked at the rock with hope. "If it's as valuable as that man said—if he buys it for—for hundreds of dollars—what we will be able to do! The Lord knows!"

MaryJake and Hannah washed up and combed their hair and made themselves presentable before walking to the settlement. They took a penny from MaryJake's bottle money to buy a postcard, and MaryJake made sure she had the man's address in her pocket. At the post office they whispered and giggled as they wrote their message in pencil. They couldn't decide how to spell "meteorite." Instead they substituted "shooting star." "He'll know what we mean," MaryJake said. They each signed it: "Miss Hannah Mowry" and "Mr. Jake Smith."

When they handed it to the post office lady she examined it. "You've addressed it fine to Mr. Dane Hollister but you need a house number on this street." MaryJake showed her the man's card. "See," the woman said. "Add this information. That way the postman can deliver it to the right place."

"When you reckon he'll get this card?" MaryJake asked, anxious to know how soon Mr. Hollister might be arriving.

"Day after tomorrow, probably." The post office lady used an ink pad and stamper to cancel their postcard and to show where and when it was mailed.

They didn't hurry on the way back to Miz Bennett's. They planned how they would spend the meteorite money.

"First thing I'll do," Hannah said, "I'll pay you what you loaned me for the tooth doctor. Then I'm going to buy my granny a silky dress, so she can feel how smooth it is. And some sweet-smelling scent. And me a new dress to go with my new teeth." She grinned at MaryJake, showing off her teeth again. "And let's gift Miss Celestine with some money to help her and Dink."

"I'm for that," MaryJake agreed. "And I want to buy a pretty thing for Miz Bennett—I can't decide what." Suddenly serious, she sat on the resting log halfway up the trail. "Hannah, most of all, I want to fetch my brothers." Hannah perched beside her and pulled a sprig of pepper grass to chew, waiting. "They're little—five and six years old. They're over in Mississippi at a place called Okolona with somebody who doesn't want them. I've got to fetch them—and then help Miz Bennett house and feed them. That's what I want most." MaryJake suddenly determined that she would tell Miz Bennett tomorrow about Paul and David. Then they could make plans for them.

"You're lucky—two brothers. I got no sisters, no brothers—only an uncle, and sometimes I wish . . ." Hannah didn't finish.

MaryJake was relieved to have told her friend a little bit of the truth about herself. And even more relieved that Hannah didn't show surprise or ask questions about her family. How could she ever explain Ma and Pa?

TWENTY·SEVEN

MR. HOLLISTER came as soon as he received their postcard, he told them when he walked out of the woods. "I left my car on the highway," he said. "I was too excited to search for a road in here. Let's see what you've found."

Miss Celestine, Miz Bennett, Hannah, and MaryJake circled him in the yard as he held the rock in his hands. They watched him examine it in the bright sun, look at every inch of it through a small magnifying lens, scrape it with his fingernail, and smell it. MaryJake squeezed her hands together, unable to bear the silence and suspense.

At last he cleared his throat. "I'm satisfied this is it. Will you show me where you found it? I'm wondering why it wasn't embedded in the ground."

Miss Celestine stayed with Miz Bennett at the cabin while Hannah and MaryJake, telling the story of how Buck found the rock, led the man along the trail. After they reached the spot, he studied the ground thoroughly and had them tell the story again. He asked questions till MaryJake and Hannah grew tired of repeating themselves.

"Something broke its fall," he decided, looking up at the treetops. He bent his neck back farther, looking higher yet to the rocky cliffs above the trees. "Perhaps it hit that rock outcropping, then bounced among these big trees. Slowed its descent. Remember that white smear on its side? That's probably from hitting the cliff."

Back at Miz Bennett's, the man said how grateful he was for all the trouble they had gone to, and he pulled a slender book out of his pocket. He flipped it open saying, "I'll write each of you a check for ten dollars. Is that satisfactory?"

"Ten dollars?" Hannah gasped.

"Just ten dollars?" MaryJake echoed Hannah. "You said it was valuable!"

Mr. Hollister looked startled. "Well, it is—valuable to science and to me for my collection, but not so much valuable in money."

"I can't believe it!" MaryJake cried. "Ten dollars is not valuable!"

"Well—well—." Mr. Hollister fidgeted with his fountain pen. "I'll make it fifteen, then." His fountain pen made a scratching sound as he filled out the checks. He ripped each paper out of his little book and handed one to Hannah—"For Miss Hannah Mowry," he said—and the other one to MaryJake—"For Mr. Jake Smith"—and he snapped his checkbook closed. "And thanks again."

After Mr. Hollister said good-bye and walked off toward the highway, those he left behind sat on the porch in deep gloom.

"Only fifteen dollars!" Hannah lamented. "My teeth cost three times that much."

"Only fifteen dollars!" MaryJake despaired. "I need three times that much for Paul and David." A remembrance flitted through her mind of the day not so long ago when she thought a quarter was a fortune, but then the memory was gone, and she didn't think of it again.

Miss Celestine jumped up and said, "Take heart. God will work it out for us."

TWENTY·EIGHT

AFTER CHORES MARYJAKE stayed at the barn while Miss Celestine went to the cabin to help with supper. She leaned on the fence for a while, listening to the animals settling in to sleep. It would be dark of the moon tonight. Already she could hardly make out Culver stretched in his straw. "Keep safe," she instructed the animals before turning toward the house. Her heart felt weighed down with disappointment and foreboding. But it was her own fault she felt that way. She should have known that life could never be as easy as she and Hannah had planned it.

Sleep didn't come willingly to MaryJake that night. When it finally eased around her like a dark fog she sank so deep that Culver's scream for help couldn't waken her immediately. Miss Celestine was already off the porch and running along the path to the barn when MaryJake in her white nightshirt came flying out of the house. They reached the empty pigpen at the same time. Culver's panic-stricken wail was fading downhill toward the creek.

MaryJake started after him but Miss Celestine held her back. "Too dangerous in the dark. We'll go tomorrow." MaryJake knew that was wise counseling, but tomorrow would be too late. On the way back to the cabin, with Miss Celestine pulling her along by the arm, MaryJake laid her plans. Miz Bennett waited at the edge of the porch. When she heard that Culver was gone she wrung her hands. "The last one! That sweet little ole boy! Oh, Jake!"

"That varmint!" MaryJake's jaw was set stiff with anger. She could hardly open her mouth. "He'll pay for this." But even as she said it she felt uneasy, remembering the neat little cabin with a yardful of jumbled wild beauty. An unlikely thief if she ever saw one. Was someone—maybe George—intentionally leading them astray?

As quickly as she could she got back on her mattress and waited for the other two to fall asleep. Then she waited even longer, not willing to risk being caught carrying out her intentions. Slithering off the corn shucks, she dressed without a sound. Peering out the door, studying Miss Celestine on her pallet, she wished for a light of some kind to help her find the way in such a darkness. She crept toward the end of the porch opposite Miss Celestine, sat on the edge, and slid off till her stretched toes touched the sand.

Once away from the house she stopped to regain her breath and to get her directions straightened out. She had to find the creek and go along it through the ruined land at top speed, hoping to reach the moon-eyed boy's house before anything happened to Culver. The thought of his terrified wail trailing off down toward the creek spurred her on.

Though her shirt and overalls were dark, MaryJake knew that without any cover her movement showed her up plain to anyone or anything watching. She felt like a rabbit fleeing from a hawk circling overhead. She paused under the crooked beech tree, looking backward and looking forward. Nothing moved either way. After a moment's rest she hurried on, past the headwaters that made a muttering noise boiling out of the ground and on to the little house.

It was silent and lightless, without anything stirring. Even in the dark she could make out some of the blossoms, and the air was layered with sweet smells. Now I'm here, what'll I do? she wondered. If I falter Culver will be lost. She strode straight for where she remembered the door to be, stepping on plants, and shrinking as she heard the crushing leaves. Culver! She must keep him in mind, no matter what she had to do to find him.

She beat on the door and screamed, "Poe! Poe Blanton! Are you home? I need help!" She hammered with both fists and begged him to answer. When she gave up and turned away, a calm voice said from the yard, "What do you want?" And there he stood. Even in the moonless night he shone silver—silver hair, silver eyebrows, and when she came closer, silver eyelashes.

MaryJake said, "Culver—my pig—have you got him?"

"No," said the calm voice. "What would I do with a pig? It would root up all my plants."

MaryJake couldn't tell what age Poe was. "Do you know where he is?"

"Probably. Being out at night I see a lot going on other folks don't know about."

"Tell me. I have to get him back quick—for Miz Bennett—for me." MaryJake couldn't believe this was the varmint she was talking to. "Are you—are you Poe?"

"Yes. And you are?"

"Jake Smith. I live with Miz Bennett." This person talked as proper as Ma did. MaryJake shivered.

"I know. My aunt Myra told me."

"She—she's your aunt?"

"Yes. She told me you fought Titus." She heard laughter in his words. "Titus is all right. But sometimes he needs sitting on."

"But why do you live here? I—I thought—" She didn't know what she meant to say.

"I live here because it's my land. My mother left it to me."

MaryJake felt dazed, unable to think. She could not understand what she was doing standing here in the middle of a wildflower garden in the dark of the moon breathing a mix of perfumes that made her head whirl and talking with a person she had never seen before, a person she wasn't really seeing now.

"Culver," she said. "I have to find him."

"Go home. I'll bring him to you tomorrow night."

MaryJake didn't believe him. How could he speak so calmly, so surely? Unless he was holding Culver captive. But Culver would have heard her voice and set up a squeal to let her know where he was. She bowed her head, thinking.

"Go home," he said.

"Are you speaking true?" she asked. "You'll bring him back?"

"Believe me."

She turned slowly away from him, from his little house, from his wildflowers. As in a dream she picked her way through the garden, smelling the mint she stepped on, the wild thyme, and the star anise. After she passed the springs and came into the barren land, she forced her feet to speed faster. Once she thought she had lost her way, but after pausing and calming down, she found it again and was home well before daybreak.

Back again in Mr. Bennett's nightshirt, safe under the Rainbow Falls quilt, she began trembling as if an ague had seized her. She couldn't understand anything of what had happened. If Poe Blanton was not the varmint, who had stolen Culver? Who was this Poe? Why did he live in the dark? Was he an albino? Myra Kirkbank Agnew was his aunt. Who was his mother? None of MaryJake's thoughts made sense.

Did Poe speak true? Would Culver be back in his pen tomorrow night? She held on to that thought and the calm surety of Poe's voice when he promised. In that way she finally fell asleep.

The next night MaryJake went to bed with her clothes on. When all was still she slipped out of the house and went to the barnyard. At first she sat atop the rail fence because she didn't want Poe to think she was sneaking and hiding. But she turned sleepy and nearly fell off. She moved to sit on the ground near Dink, who was lying with his knees folded under him, and there she did fall asleep. She became aware of movement and awoke to see Poe entering the barnyard with Culver in his arms. Dink was awake and watching but he stayed where he was. MaryJake pulled herself up, holding onto the pigpen.

"Here he is," Poe said in his calm voice. "As good as ever except he's hungry."

MaryJake reached for the pig. "I've got some cracked corn for him and some chufa nuts." She patted him and hugged him. Culver was not like a dog in his greeting. He acted as if he had known all along he would be brought home safely so there was no need making a fuss about it. MaryJake laughed, then set him down in his pen. While he munched and grunted, she said, "I'm ever so much obliged to you. And Miz Bennett is too. I told her you would be bringing him back."

"She was surprised?"

"Not Miz Bennett. But Hannah didn't believe it."

He laughed. "Hannah would not want to know who stole your pig."

"What you say tells me that I would not want her to know. She's my friend—and she loves her uncle George."

"Why were you and Hannah in my yard?"

"How did you know?" MaryJake bit her tongue, but not soon enough. He seemed so normal she forgot that he wasn't.

"I heard you."

"We were looking for the meteorite. The one that fell. A man offered to buy it when we found it."

"Did you find it?" He leaned over and scratched around his ankles with both hands.

"We found it. I mean, Hannah's calf, Buck, found it." MaryJake thought of their lost fortune. "Hannah was going to pay for her teeth and I was going to—" She hesitated. It seemed so easy in the dark to say things that were hard to say at other times. "I was going to fetch my little brothers."

She told him where they were and why she needed to go for them.

Poe had propped his left foot on the pen and bent over still scratching. "You never know what might turn up," he said. "Surprises happen all the time."

Watching him tonight MaryJake realized he was not grown up. More than sixteen, she thought, but not much more. "What's the matter—did poison ivy catch you?"

"A double case of it," he said, scratching his other ankle. "Poison ivy is the itchingest itch there is. I can't always recognize it in the dark. Aunt Myra gave me something from the drugstore that helps a little."

MaryJake said slowly, "If Myra is your aunt, who is your mother?"

"Once there were three beautiful Kirkbank sisters—Myra, Adelia, and my mother, Caroline."

"Caroline," MaryJake said stupidly. "I never heard of her."

"You've heard of the other two then?" He turned to look at her.

"Well, well—I've seen Myra," MaryJake stuttered. "And maybe heard tell of—of Adelia." How hard it was to say Ma's name.

"Adelia left home a long time ago," he said. "And my mother died before Adelia left. How did you hear of them?"

MaryJake's mind was churning. "I can't remember exactly. I have to go now. Much obliged for Culver." She whirled and almost ran toward the house.

When she reached the shadow of the porch, she looked back. She could see the silver of his hair as he stood at the barnyard fence.

Next day MaryJake said to Hannah, "I want to hunt a flower that I know about—lady's-earing, it's called. It makes a good salve for poison ivy. We can set it out in the garden."

"That's something Granny needs to know about. Once in a while she gets into a patch of ivy, not being able to see."

They took two rusty buckets from the barn and a shovel. "It grows alongside branches like the one from Miz Bennett's spring," MaryJake said, leading the way. "In the shade."

They waded in the stream, searching on both sides.

"I had poison ivy real bad one time," Hannah said. "My eyes swolled up till I couldn't see out of 'em. Granny had to tie my hands behind my back to keep me from scratching. It was near as bad as the toothache."

"It must be awful," MaryJake said, remembering how Poe couldn't control his scratching.

She found what they were looking for at a bend of the stream in deep shade. The plants, spangled with orange and brown deep-throated flowers, leaned over the stream. "Look, Hannah," she said, and shook one of the stems. All the bright flowers, swinging from what looked like a thread, danced like a lady's earring.

Hannah laughed and shook another bush. "They're sure pretty," she said.

MaryJake chose the ones to dig. As they worked she said, "One for your grandma, one for Miz Bennett, and I'm going to take one to Poe Blanton."

Hannah straightened, staring at MaryJake in surprise. "The varmint? What for? I'd be skeered to go back there."

"I'm not scared. I don't believe he's the varmint. And he needs it for his yard."

"All that stuff he's growing there—how you know he's not already got it?"

"I didn't see it, and I looked hard at everything. His garden's a real blue-ribbon prize, but I didn't see any lady's-earing in it." MaryJake packed the woodsy dirt around the roots of each plant. "See, we'll give him this biggest, prettiest one. A gift has to be the best. Ours will be these two in the same bucket." She watered the plants thoroughly.

They took the shovel back to the barn.

"You needn't go with me if you don't want to," MaryJake said. "I'm going to write a note." She tore a piece off of a paper bag Miz Bennett had in the feed room and took a length of string from the nail. At the cabin she found a pencil nub in the drawer of Miz Bennett's sewing machine and wrote on the paper, "lady's-earing—boil leaves and flowers and apply juice to poison ivy." She used the string to tie the note on the bucket.

Though Hannah said this was a flighty thing to be doing, she didn't want to be left behind. She hiked with MaryJake to the headwaters of Yellow Bird Creek and stayed under the shelter of the trees while MaryJake crossed the yard. It was more beautiful than she remembered. She paused in the middle, turning slowly in every direction and breathing in deep, trying to separate the mixed fragrances. She had never seen such masses of wild blue phlox. They bordered the porch and seemed like part of the early morning sky come down to earth. Poe's well house had baskets of ferns hanging from the ceiling, every kind MaryJake knew and several she didn't know.

She realized she still held the gift plant. She decided to set the bucket near the front door, adjusting the note and making sure it was secure. Then they made the trek back to Miz Bennett's, where they planted MaryJake's flower in a corner of the garden, and Hannah carried hers home in the bucket.

TWENTY·NINE

EVERY NIGHT SINCE she left the plant on his porch, MaryJake had watched for Poe to come to Culver's pen. She didn't see him, though, until the moon was waxing, and combined its light with the starshine to pick up the silver of his hair.

"I'm going out to check the animals," she said to Miz Bennett and Miss Celestine, and she left them sitting on the porch.

He was watching for her. "Thanks for the remedy— my poison ivy's nearly cured. Your plant's called jewel-weed, too. Did you know? My aunt Myra looked it up for me."

"No, but I see why. The flowers are like jewels."

"I would have come to thank you before, but I go certain nights to Aunt Myra's—she teaches me."

"Oh, I wondered. You talk . . . educated."

"I'd like to meet Miz Bennett and Miss Celestine. May I?"

MaryJake felt suddenly shy and wordless. She held on to the barnyard rail, trying to sort out her thoughts. "This—this is Miss Celestine's horse, Dink," she said foolishly, reaching out to pat Dink's soft nose, touching his loose lips. "But I don't know—are you sure—will it be all right for you to be at our house?"

"Why not? I can't see any harm done. Then I can come to your porch at night and visit with you. I'm a little like Titus—curious about who you are, what you are."

MaryJake stiffened. That stuck-up Titus! He had accused her of being a gypsy boy, of fighting like a girl. She hadn't forgotten. Here was dangerous ground. But Poe didn't seem to be a threat at the moment—he spoke in a funning way. And she would like to know him better and find out about his work with the wildflowers. Lately she had been thinking she could be a plant person, but more than a gardener, someone who knew everything about all the plants in the world, how to grow them and how to use them in doctoring.

She beckoned him to follow her and led the way to the porch. The two women were startled, but they made Poe welcome. He took the chair they offered, and the three of them did all of the talking while MaryJake sat on the steps listening.

After that first night, Poe came over whenever he could—at least once a week—to visit on the porch. He was interested to hear all about Miss Celestine's mission and to consider with her and Miz Bennett what the exploding of the meteorite meant.

"I'm wondering if it was a sign from God that it's time for me and ole Dink to move on," Miss Celestine said in an uncertain voice. "Nothing like that's ever happened to me before." MaryJake thought how much she and Miz Bennett and Hannah would miss her company if she left.

Miz Bennett confided one night when Poe sat with them on the porch that she longed to restore the old graveyard in the clearing, mend the broken tombstones, pull out the weeds, and let the roses run wild all over the graves and the iron fence. "My gran'pa and gran'ma are buried there. I don't remember 'xactly where 'cause they don't have a marker excepting sand rocks. I wish I could make the graveyard prettier for them."

Poe talked about his longing to buy and reforest the cutover land between Miz Bennett's place and his own. "I believe when the creek waters run clear again, the deer and the squirrel will return. And who knows? The small parrots might come back again." MaryJake wondered if that desolate acreage could ever come alive, but Poe sounded as confident as when he had assured MaryJake that he would bring Culver home.

He always tried to draw MaryJake into the conversation. She never had much to say but she enjoyed listening to their deepest dreams and wonderings. And an idea grew in her mind—she realized that she had, tied in the corner of Ma's lacy handkerchief, the means to make their dreams come true as well as her own. With the meteorite money Hannah had insisted on paying to MaryJake, plus what was left from the bottle fund, she had enough money to go for Paul and David. But she needed more money to build a lean-to against the side of Miz Bennett's house to accomodate them.

MaryJake felt giddy thinking of the power of that ring.

One morning she stuffed the handkerchief in her overall pocket and invited Miss Celestine to walk to the clearing with her. They sat on the overturned tombstone. MaryJake cleared her throat, not knowing how to begin. She pulled the handkerchief out of her pocket, laid it between them, and said without preliminaries, "I want you to sell this for me. Maybe you know somebody in town who would buy it. Then we can divide the money, you, Miz Bennett, Poe, and me."

Puzzled, Miss Celestine untied the knot. She took one look and let go of the handkerchief as if it were poison. "Where did you get this?" Her eyes looked big as moonflowers.

When MaryJake didn't answer, Miss Celestine said, "I don't mean to accuse you. But—but I never saw such a ring. Is it yours by right?" She clasped her hands together and chewed her lips. "Forgive me, MaryJake. I don't know what I'm saying."

"The ring was an honest gift to me—from Ma. But I don't choose to accept it. All I want is enough money to build a lean-to for Paul and David onto Miz Bennett's house. You all can have the rest."

Miss Celestine looked searchingly at MaryJake, then at the ring. "It's beautiful—the most beautiful piece of jewelry I ever saw. Old and valuable, I'm sure."

"It must not be connected with me in any way."

"You know I'll have to ask God about this, MaryJake—er, Jake. Shall I keep it till then?"

MaryJake nodded. "Now I have to get back to help Miz Bennett in the garden." And she left Miss Celestine staring at the diamond where it lay on the handkerchief.

God must have assured Miss Celestine the ring was all right because next day she had it in the pocket of her dress-up dress—the lace peeked out. MaryJake asked no questions. She took for granted that Miss Celestine was on her way to catch the town bus to sell the ring. MaryJake had no regrets about it, but went to bring water from the spring, do the barn chores, and work over the garden. She didn't see Miss Celestine again until the three of them sat down to supper. She did not seem changed in any way. MaryJake felt that if she had sold the ring for a huge sum something about her would show it. She prepared herself for disappointment.

But she was in for a greater shock than she suspected. The three of them were sitting quietly on the porch in the dark, not expecting Poe as this was one of his school nights with his aunt Myra, but he came walking up the hill from the creek. After greetings, he settled himself in his usual place, but then he said in his easy way, "I found your note, Miss Celestine, with the package. They took me by surprise. Please don't be offended, but I need to know how you came by that ring."

MaryJake felt hit by a thunderclap. Miss Celestine hadn't gone to town to sell the ring. She had gone to Poe! MaryJake didn't know she even knew the way to Poe's house. She held her breath. The porch was so quiet they could hear Dink blow his lips in the barnyard.

Miss Celestine said slowly, "I cannot tell you anything about the ring other than I came by it honestly. As I wrote in my note, I want your advice about selling it. Why do you need to know how I got it?"

Poe said just as slowly, "Because there were three of

those rings, exactly alike. The father of my great-great grandmother and her two sisters designed the rings for his daughters. In each generation since then three girls in the Kirkbank family have worn those rings. There are no others like them. Now my aunt Myra has one, and I have Caroline's because she was my mother. So yours must be Adelia's. But where is Adelia?"

Finally in the silence, MaryJake spoke. "Did you truly know Adelia?" She hadn't meant for her voice to sound so forlorn.

"Yes. I was seven years old when she left, just after my mother died from infantile paralysis." MaryJake's back was to him but from the sound of his voice she knew he was leaning toward her. "Adelia left with a sharecropper named Wildsmith."

MaryJake's head was bowed onto her knees. She felt like covering her ears with her hands. She did not want Poe's quiet voice to continue. She feared what she might hear.

"I loved Aunt Adelia. I've wondered so often where she went, what happened to her, if her marriage was happy. I've wondered about other things too." He hesitated. "You see, when she left she took my sister with her, my little green-eyed towheaded sister."

MaryJake leaped to her feet. "You're lying, Poe Blanton! And I won't hear another word!" She stomped into the house, jerked off her clothes in the dark, flung on her night-shirt without buttoning it, and pulled the Rainbow Falls quilt over her head. She did not know what Poe's words meant. She did not want to know what they meant. She cried into Miz Bennett's feather pillow until she fell asleep.

THIRTY

MARYJAKE REFUSED to think about the things Poe had said. She knew none of it was true. "I belong to Ma and Pa," she said over and over to herself. "Paul and David are my brothers. Ma, Pa, Paul, and David—they are my family." She would not consider any other possibility, even though her parents had abandoned her by the side of the road.

She resolved to go for her brothers as soon as she could get ready. Miz Bennet was anxious for her to bring them "home." Miss Celestine and Miz Bennett washed her overalls and shirt in homemade soap and hung them on bushes at the spring to dry. MaryJake stayed indoors in Mr. Bennett's shirt to make her lunch, putting in extra for Paul and David. Miss Celestine cut her hair and wrote directions for finding the Wildsmith place.

"Don't go into Okolona," Miss Celestine said. "That's too far. Tell the bus driver where you want off. He'll help you."

Though MaryJake went in her overalls and bare feet,

everything about her was clean. Hannah walked to the highway with her, insisting on carrying the lunch sack, and watched her board the bus. MaryJake looked back just in time to catch a yearning expression on her face, which Hannah quickly erased with a wide smile. MaryJake, for a moment, wished it were Hannah going instead of herself, but then she thought of Paul and David and waved.

The bus ride was thrilling, speeding down the road, with MaryJake looking over the driver's shoulder, seeing everything ahead and on both sides of the road at the same time. They stopped at bus stations in little towns, and they stopped along the road when people waved them down. Some of them had suitcases and boxes. Others, like MaryJake, carried only a brown paper bag. She studied everyone with interest, wondering where they were going and why.

The driver announced when they crossed the Mississippi state line. MaryJake was disappointed to see that Mississippi looked no different from Alabama. She sat on the edge of her seat wondering if he would forget to put her off at the right place. Finally she cleared her throat and said just behind the driver's ear, "You remember about the Wildsmith place, don't you? Just outside Okolona?"

The driver lifted his cap to let the air cool his head, glanced in the mirror above him and said, "Yeah, son, I remember. Don't know what I'd do with you in Okolona if I forgot."

The wind whipped through the rolled-down bus windows, slapping MaryJake in the face with live bugs that fell in her lap. She tossed them out the window again, past the woman beside her who leaned to one side and held onto her hat.

The bus driver put her out by the side of the road at what looked like a junkyard of rusty cans, old cars, and farm machinery. Standing uncertainly on the ground, looking up at the driver, she said, "When will a bus be going back to Rock Castle tomorrow?"

"Passes here about ten o'clock."

"Watch for me," MaryJake said anxiously. "Me and two little boys."

The driver nodded, shut the door, and rumbled off.

MaryJake walked up the dirt lane to a house covered with a rusty tin roof. A wide dogtrot ran through the middle with a room on each side. Two bony hounds lay asleep in the dog trot. Playing under the house, which slumped on brick stilts, was a towheaded boy—Paul. MaryJake went toward him and called his name. The child glanced up at her, but continued pouring sand back and forth from one tin can to another. All the while he hummed "Barbrie Allen" as if he were a wheezy organ pumping out the tune in a big hurry with no end in sight.

MaryJake knelt down and reached for him. "Paul, it's me, MaryJake. I've come for you." He continued pouring sand and humming as if she were not there, even after she drew him from under the house into her lap. "Paul, where's David? Show MaryJake where David is." She gently took the cans out of his hands and stood him up in her arms trying to get his attention. He felt thin, his eyes looked vague and his hair was matted and shaggy. "Where is your brother?" He gave no sign that he heard her.

MaryJake set him on the edge of the porch, his feet dangling. She took a red all-day sucker out of the lunch bag and peeled away the cover. "Look what MaryJake brought you. And I've got one for David too."

Paul put the candy in his mouth and pointed a dirty finger toward the corner of the house. MaryJake went around the corner. She found David asleep on the ground in the chimney corner, his thumb in his mouth. She picked him up so easily he didn't awaken at first and took him to where she had left Paul. The three of them sat there, with MaryJake talking about everything she could think of from the past, trying to stir some response. No recognition showed in David's eyes. He accepted the candy and quietly gnawed on it. The boys were here beside her, one on each side, yet they were absent.

MaryJake slipped the lunch bag into the bib of her overalls as a truck rattled into the yard and parked. She watched a man and woman get out. The man was enough like Pa that she knew he must be his brother. The woman, carrying a sack of groceries, glanced at them and went into the house by way of the dogtrot.

THIRTY·ONE

THE MAN SAID, "Well, well. It's time somebody showed up to take these little rascals off my hands. I done the best I could for 'em, the very best, but enough is enough, don't you know. You MaryJake?"

She nodded, not offering to shake his hand.

"I've heerd 'bout you," her uncle said. He wagged his head and gave a disgusted sigh. "These boys is a real responsibility, no two ways 'bout it. Extra mouths to feed, and grub is scarce. I ain't able to work, and neither is Troonie. It's just hand to mouth for us. And I ain't heerd a word from your ma and pa, not one word. They said they'd send money just as soon as they could, but not one cent's come." He whined worse than Culver.

"I've come to take them away," MaryJake said. "I'll pay you for their keep. And mine too if I can stay the night. We'll catch the bus tomorrow at ten o'clock."

"Well, you know po' as I am I can't put you up for free. Your pa swore he'd come back for 'em soon as ever he could. How much money you got?"

"Enough to pay you what's right."

The woman called him, and he grumbled something before going inside. MaryJake walked about the yard with the boys, looking at flowering weeds, butterflies, worms, and bugs, trying every way she could to reach them. They went with her, looked at what she pointed out, even let her hold their hands, but they stayed silent.

Finally she asked them to take her inside the house where the woman and man were. The woman had white bread slices spread out on the table. She was slapping mustard on them and then laying pieces of bologna meat on the bread. The man was working with an old kerosene stove, trying to light the wick under a coffeepot.

"Can I help you do something?" MaryJake asked.

The woman looked at her but said nothing. The man said, "Naw, naw. Y'all sit down. You're paying guests. You don't have to work like us po' folks." He sniggered.

"We'll wash up," MaryJake said, "if you'll show me where."

The woman pointed the long butcher knife toward the backyard. MaryJake found a well there. She drew up a bucket of yellow water and poured it in a pan on the well shelf. She looked around for soap but found none. From her overall pocket she pulled out Ma's lace handkerchief to use as a washing rag. The boys were sweaty and dirty, and she felt dusty herself. She joked with them about the dirt necklace in the fold of their necks. They used to laugh together about that, but not now. They let her wash them as she wanted—not resisting, but not helping.

When they returned to the kitchen, the man and woman were seated at the table, eating. The coffee smelled good as it boiled on the stove. MaryJake would have liked a cup but she didn't dare ask for it. Three squares of wax paper were laid on the table for them, and on each paper was half of a bologna sandwich. An open box of Fig Newtons centered the table.

"Pull up a chair," the man said. "Hep yourself."

In the silence MaryJake could hear the man chewing. She noticed he had two sandwiches, whole ones, and the woman ate a whole and a half. As soon as she took the first bite, MaryJake's stomach began growling, demanding more food, faster. But she knew there would be no more, and only one Fig Newton each.

MaryJake offered to help wash the supper things, but the man refused. He gave her a thin quilt and showed her where to spread it in the dogtrot. As soon as dark came she and the boys lay down on their pallet in their clothes. She hadn't seen a timepiece anywhere, but somehow she had to know when ten o'clock came tomorrow. She could hardly wait to board the bus with her brothers and take them away from here.

She told the boys stories as they waited for sleep. She told them their old favorite about the animals that ran away from unhappy homes to go to Bremen. "And that's where we're going tomorrow—to Bremen," she whispered. She named Miz Bennett's animals and described them and told the boys how happy the animals would be to have Paul and David live with them. The boys didn't respond. They lay quietly and went to sleep without answering her in any way.

MaryJake was still awake when one of the dogs walked onto their quilt. It turned round and round and then sank

down with a groan that reminded her of ole Dink. Homesickness came up from her stomach, from her heart, making her throat ache and her eyes burn. She resolved that
tomorrow, first thing, before the man and woman were up,
she'd take the boys and go. They'd walk along the road
toward home until the bus caught up with them. Pa could
settle the boys' bill with his brother later.

She was up before daylight, waking the boys and washing them and herself at the well. She folded the quilt and
laid it on a chair in the dogtrot. Then they sat on the steps
and ate a peanut butter sandwich from her sack before
starting their trip. She was leading them out of the yard
toward the road when the man came round the corner of
the house.

"Caught you!" he said. "Sneakin' out that way ain't
proper. After all I done for these here boys you is honor
bound to recompense me. I ain't lookin' for full payment,
you understand. Money couldn't repay me for all I done for
those two."

The boys stood beside MaryJake, showing neither fear
nor dislike, only that state of absence. "How much are you
charging?" MaryJake asked.

"Well, the two of 'em been here over three months, I
figure, maybe four, eatin' us out o'house and home. Besides
their doctor bills, the clothes I had to buy for 'em, haircuts ever' two weeks, and keepin' their clothes washed and
mended—they're rough boys, you know, hard on clothes.
They tear a good shirt to rags the first time they wear it.
Well, I figure a hunderd dollars would be jus' a fraction of
what they done cost me."

"A hundred dollars! I don't have a hundred dollars."

"Then I'm just afeerd they ain't going anywhere. Not till their pa comes and pays their bill in full." He encircled the boys with his stringy but strong-looking arms. "Nope. They ain't takin' a step out o'this yard till full payment's made."

MaryJake's heart shrank as he herded the boys toward the house. So near to escaping! How could she have failed! If the boys disappeared into that house she would never see them again.

"Wait! Wait!" she cried pulling the lump of bills out of her pocket. "I don't have a hundred. This is all, every bit of what I have." She held it out to him. In spite of a strong effort to control herself, tears rolled down her cheeks.

"Well," he said taking the bills, unfolding them in one hand and caressing them with the other. "I see a twenty here, and a ten, some ones, and a five. Maybe I can make do with this." He glanced up at her, his eyes greedy bright.

"It's our bus fare," MaryJake said. "It's all I have to get us home."

"You'll make out all right, I'm sure of that. Smart girl like you'll think o'somethin'. Now git on your way."

MaryJake kept standing there, holding the boys close to her, looking to their uncle for some mercy.

"Git! I said. Rattler, King! Sic 'em!"

MaryJake didn't fear the old bony hounds. But when they came running, growling in their throats, she changed her mind and hurried the boys away toward the road.

THIRTY-TWO

THEY HAD BEEN walking two hours at least, and the sun was burning hot when she heard the bus coming. The driver must have recognized them because he tooted his horn. MaryJake looked over her shoulder, her eyes blinded with tears, and shook her head at him to say no. When the bus swept past, spewing enough exhaust fumes to make them cough, MaryJake led the boys off the road to the shade of a bush. She wiped her eyes on her shirttail and hugged her knees while the little boys squatted and drew lines in the sand with their fingers. Before starting out again they each chewed a slice of Miz Bennett's dried apples. The lunch sack was nearly flat now.

The boys did not speak a word, not even to complain of thirst. An hour or so more and she found a spring in a shady place a little distance off the highway. Cars had worn a road to it, and a gourd dipper hung on a tree over the water. They drank, and MaryJake wet the handkerchief in the runoff to wash their flushed faces. She persuaded the boys to wade a while before leading them back to the highway.

About midday a rusty car rattled to a stop on the shoulder and a grizzle-bearded man stuck his head out the window. "I'm going thirty mile or so ahead. Hop in if that suits you." MaryJake didn't waste a thought on whether this man was an Evildoer or not. She was too glad to get off the hot road and rest their feet for a while. The man opened the door and they climbed in the backseat. A spotted hound sat on the passenger side of the front seat. It never turned its head to look at MaryJake and the boys. The man didn't talk, which suited MaryJake. The hot wind whipped around them, the scenery passed, and too soon he said, "This is as far as I go." MaryJake thanked him, and they began walking again.

When they came to a country store, MaryJake went in to ask for a drink of water for the boys. The woman directed them to a hydrant at the side of the store. She spoke in a kind way, which gave MaryJake courage to ask if they could sit on the bench in the shade of the store porch and rest a while. "Make yourself at home," the woman said. MaryJake opened the lunch sack and handed around chufa nuts till the sack was empty. She folded it with care and slipped it in her pocket.

The woman came outside and sat with them. "Lots of people traveling," she said, fanning herself with a paper sack. "It's real sad what a hard time folks are having. I hope you're not on the road after dark. Where're you headed?"

MaryJake told her.

"Gee, you still got a long way to go. I'd hate for my boys to . . ." Her voice trailed off.

MaryJake didn't want her to feel bad for them. "Yes, ma'am. We'll be all right."

As soon as they finished eating the chufas and drank more water, they were off again. MaryJake tried singing Ma's ballads to pass the time. She had sung every one she could remember when a hay truck stopped. "You can ride back there with the hay," a young man yelled from the driver's window. MaryJake helped the boys up into the bed of the truck and they made themselves comfortable on the sweet-smelling hay. The boys were asleep and the sun was near setting when the truck turned in at a farm driveway. The young man came around to the back to help them down. "Good luck," he said, and drove toward the farmhouse.

As they set out again, MaryJake once more began the story of the animals running away to Bremen, and how they found the rich house full of food and every comfort, and how they frightened the robbers out of the house with their loud cries. MaryJake then made the sound of every one of Miz Bennett's animals in turn, and she named each one until she came to the chickens, turkeys, geese, and guineas. For them she made only their sounds because there were so many of them she couldn't keep their names straight. She saved the peafowl's cry till last because it was so terrifying. She didn't remember that a peafowl went to Bremen in the original story, but she put one in her story for the awful effect. The bedtime cries of Miz Bennett's peafowl would put the fear of God into the most wicked Evildoer.

THIRTY·THREE

S HE HAD FINISHED the story, and they were walking along with MaryJake wondering if her brothers
would ever come alive again, when a combination car and
truck—the back had a sort of little house built on it but the
front was like a regular car—stopped and waited for them.
A man about as old as Pa got out as they neared his vehicle. "Hey, you boys want a ride?" he called. MaryJake for
the first time felt uneasy. She held tight to the boys' hands
and stared at the man. Oh, how she longed to get in and
sink back in the seat and let the miles fly, fly away under
the wheels! But he was different from the others they had
ridden with, more citylike, and she couldn't decide what
to do.

He must have read indecision in her face because he
said, "It's all right. The lady back at the store told me to
watch for y'all. Said you're going to Rock Castle. Happens I
pass right by there if you want to go with me."

MaryJake was too tired and relieved to express the joy
she felt. "Much obliged," she said. He directed MaryJake to

get in and then he lifted David and placed him in her lap and fitted Paul beside her and shut the door.

The man was proud of his vehicle. He told MaryJake about it as he pushed the accelerator pedal nearly flat on the floor. "I built it myself, to hold my samples. I'm a salesman and I drive around in Mississippi and Alabama visiting country stores and taking orders. I've got space in the back where I can sleep if I have to. Most of the time though folks invite me to stay with them. They like to hear news from other places and learn what's going on in the world. They're so far out in the sticks I'm sort of their entertainment. These stores along here close up before dark. I'll stop and visit with them on my way back."

The boys fell asleep. MaryJake felt mesmerized, listening to the man's voice, with the sound of the motor and the singing of the tires on the road filling in the background. She was glad he didn't ask questions. She couldn't have formed the words to answer. It seemed that all he needed was an audience and she was glad enough to furnish him with one.

In the dark she couldn't tell anything about the kind of country they were driving through, but she became alert when she noticed him looking on both sides of the road as if searching for something.

"What is it?" she asked.

"We're in your home county now. Won't be long till Rock Castle. Guess you'll be glad of it."

MaryJake leaned forward to see better through the windshield. She described the place he should put them out so they could take the path through the woods to Miz Bennett's.

"I'd feel better if I took y'all to the house," he said.

MaryJake explained about Miz Bennett not having a road. Straining to look ahead, she recognized the place where the bus had stopped for her.

"That's it—just ahead," she said. "And I'm much obliged."

"You're welcome," he said, coming around to help the boys out. MaryJake could hardly make her legs work, she had sat so long with the boys' weight on her.

"It's mighty dark," the man said looking at the woods.

A shadow moved from beneath the trees. Starshine glinted on silver hair.

"I've come for them, thanks." Poe's easy voice came like a blessing to MaryJake's weary ears.

"We're home," she said, putting into her voice her joy at seeing him.

Poe picked up Paul, and MaryJake carried David. They set their feet on her path through the clearing.

"Miz Bennett and Miss Celestine are waiting on the porch," he said. "Hannah too. They've met every bus that came from Mississippi today. Then I took over after sunset. And here you are."

"And I'm so glad. Is everybody all right?"

"Everybody's fine, even Culver." He hefted Paul. "These are two dandy boys you've brought back. Which one is which?"

MaryJake told him and explained why they hadn't returned home by bus. By then they were out of the woods, and those waiting on the porch saw them coming and hurried to meet them.

THIRTY-FOUR

EVERY NIGHT the little boys slept with MaryJake on the corn shuck mattress. She sang them to sleep with the old songs or told them a story. They went with her and Miss Celestine to do the chores, night and morning. After midday dinner Miz Bennett rocked with them in her rocking chair, an arm around each one, while they napped. Whenever Poe joined them on the porch after supper, Paul and David sat on his knees while he told them about things he had seen happen in his woods at night.

It was a great day when Hannah taught them how to ride Buck and Bennie. MaryJake could hardly contain her joy when the boys laughed as they held on to the calves by fistsful of fur. She had not felt so hopeful since she brought them home. Little by little Paul and David seemed to be thawing.

Then one night as she put them to bed, Paul took her hand and said, "Bremen," and she told them the story of Bremen again. The next day in the barnyard, one of the baby calves mooed. Both boys mooed back and laughed.

MaryJake felt sure that now they were on the way to recovery.

Poe had decided to restore the graveyard as a gift to Miz Bennett. He worked at the clearing during the nights. Sometimes MaryJake joined him and helped weed, mend tombstones, and straighten the iron fence. The rough work required heavy gloves and sharp clippers. MaryJake did not want to be with Poe for fear of what he might ask or say, but she couldn't keep away.

They talked about wild plants. He said he wanted to learn more about their medicinal uses. She offered to teach him what she knew. She told him about Miss Blackwell and the plant book and how she and her teacher had planned to make a wild garden at school before she had to move away from Three Notch. He told her how he had spent years collecting the plants for his wild garden. He said he wanted to be a botanist and grow plants in a greenhouse year round. It seemed they would never come to the point where they had nothing to say to each other, but one night their talk died out.

After a long silence he said, "Have you thought about what I told you that night before you went for the boys?"

"I don't remember," MaryJake lied. She didn't ask him to refresh her memory but he did anyway.

"About Adelia taking my little sister away with her."

"Did she kidnap her?"

"No. The family wanted Adelia to have her."

MaryJake made an elaborate shrug so he wouldn't miss seeing her indifference. "I don't know anything about your sister."

"What's your name?" Poe asked carefully.

MaryJake hesitated. She sensed a trap but couldn't identify it. "You know my name—Jake Smith."

"My sister's name was MaryJake Blanton."

MaryJake said nothing.

Poe continued pulling weeds and clipping briars. "It doesn't take much figuring to know that Adelia would have changed your name, maybe to MaryJake Wildsmith. Then you might have changed it, for some reason, to Jake Smith. But why did you come back here? And where is Adelia? I can't figure that." He shook his head.

MaryJake whacked at a sprout growing out of Millard's grave, making a deal of noise. Why was she staying with him if what he said upset her?

Because, plain and simple, she knew he was talking about something that had to be settled, something that had to be solved before her life could go on. She had either to become herself again, a girl named MaryJake Wildsmith, daughter of Adelia Kirkbank Wildsmith and her husband, or become the self she never knew she was, a girl who was the daughter of Caroline Kirkbank Blanton and a sister to Poe. Until she faced the facts, nothing could ever be right.

Poe sounded as if he were thinking out loud. "You're twelve, going on thirteen. You're towheaded and green eyed. Everything fits, except for one big item—you claim you're a boy."

"Paul and David are my brothers."

"Are you ashamed to have me for your brother?" She heard the smile in his voice.

"I'd love to have you for my brother, if I didn't have to be your sister." She shaded her voice with sarcasm. "Probably Kirkbanks don't use that word, 'love.'"

"A few Kirkbanks do. My mother, for one, Myra, for another, and Adelia."

MaryJake thought about Ma and Pa. "They didn't love me. They pushed me out of the car like a dog they didn't want. They didn't say a word of good-bye."

"Some people care," Poe said, raking the briars in a pile. "They just don't know how to show it."

The angry tears MaryJake refused to shed made her cough. Her gloved hands kept the clippers busy whacking the brush. Poe raked and stacked what they had cut and leaned his tools against the gate post. He took MaryJake's clippers and pulled off her gloves and laid them by the other tools. Then he grasped her hand and led her, resisting, to sit beside him on the overturned tombstone.

"Listen," he said. "For your own sake, you must forgive them. I know Adelia—she would do the best she could for you."

MaryJake covered her face with her hands and sobbed, "They didn't even say good-bye."

Poe put his arms around her. "Tell me," he said.

She told him, crying into his rough work shirt—the disappearance of Rose, the loss of Adder, the abandonment beside the road, the resolve to be a boy and dyeing herself in the black walnut stump—she relived it all. He said nothing, but when she moved away from him to dry her tears on her sleeves, he let her go.

"You smell good—like a cypress swamp," she said, sniffling.

Poe laughed. "Spoken like a true botanist, thank you. I know how good a cypress swamp smells." He sat silent a while. "And thank you for telling me the truth. There's no way I can make you know what it means to me to have you back. I never forgot you. And you've brought two little brothers with you!"

They stored the tools and the lantern in the temporary shed Poe had built and walked in silence to Miz Bennett's house. Everyone was already in bed. Poe took her hand and squeezed it, and they parted without words.

THIRTY-FIVE

OFTEN NOW HANNAH walked her grandma down from the ridge to sit on Miz Bennett's porch after supper. Shy with her at first, the boys soon learned she was another person to tell stories and to talk and to fun with them. The old lady seemed transformed from the person MaryJake first knew when George was in the penitentiary. A special bond developed between Hannah's grandma and Poe. Poe brought her herbs for her garden and night-blooming flowers with the sweetest fragrance he could find.

MaryJake had thought many times of what Poe said and what she had admitted that night at the graveyard. Always, she came back to Ma's troubling words: *You've got to remember, there're certain tasks in life a person has to do. Hard tasks. There's no other way, just no other way.* She knew as sure as the sun would rise tomorrow that she had the hard task of straightening out her life. But she could not bring herself to do it.

Paul did it for her. On a night when they were all

gathered on Miz Bennett's porch, the hour grew late. MaryJake was reluctant to leave the group to put the boys to bed though she knew they were tired. Paul yawned, slid off Poe's knee, and came to her. Holding his arms up he said, "Bed, Sister." He used the old pet name for the first time since the family separated.

MaryJake hugged him and said into the silence, "Yes, I'm his sister. I never meant to deceive anyone, not for this long anyway. But I was mad and hurt when I came because my parents didn't want me. I vowed not to want them."

Nobody spoke. She saw no sign of what they felt toward her. "I changed my name because I thought MaryJake Wildsmith was tacky. I turned myself into a boy because people think boys are better than girls." She hesitated, realizing she could never say all that she wanted to say. "Anyway, I'm not a boy, and I'm sorry if you're disappointed in me."

Poe continued rocking the sleeping David, and Miss Celestine, who knew so much about everybody, said nothing. MaryJake held her breath, waiting.

"I never suspected," Miz Bennett said, "but I can't say I'm disappointed."

"I'm not disappointed," Hannah said. "I'd rather you'd be a girl."

Hannah's grandma said, "A girl's as good as a boy— look at Hanner."

As long as she had finally started her confession, MaryJake determined to finish it. "Poe says I'm his sister. That means I belong in a different family, and Paul and David are not my brothers. But seems like I can't accept that I'm part of my true family till I work things out about my untrue family—and I mean untrue in more ways than one." MaryJake heard the bitterness in her voice. "That day they put me out of the car—they didn't even say good-bye. They weren't even sorry to leave me. 'Here's where you get out, MaryJake,' he said. 'Be an obedient child, MaryJake,' she said. And they went off and left me."

Miss Celestine said, "She must have loved you. She sent her precious ring to prove you were you and to pay for your keep."

Poe paused in his rocking. "Wouldn't it have been harder if they had cried? Quick and clean—wasn't that the best way?"

Paul was asleep now, leaving MaryJake free to snarl, "You can talk—the family chose you, the boy, and sent me off."

"But I was seven," Poe protested. "I could look after myself. You were only two. You needed lots of care. And, don't forget, Adelia wanted you. Adelia loved you."

MaryJake bit her lip and blinked the tears out of her eyes.

"Besides," Poe said, "accepting that I'm your brother doesn't mean you have to give up Paul and David. I'm your *oldest* brother."

MaryJake laid Paul in Miss Celestine's lap and went inside to light the lamp on the dresser. She made the bed and got out the small nightgowns that Miz Bennett and Miss Celestine had sewed on the pedal machine. Poe and Miss Celestine changed the boys' clothes on the porch and MaryJake took them in to bed.

When she came out, Hannah and her grandma had gone and Poe was leaving. He put his arm around her and said, "Keep struggling with it, little sister. You'll win out."

She didn't reply. While she unfolded Miss Celestine's

quilts, she listened to him whistling on his way toward the creek. He made it clear he believed she would come out on top of her problems, and MaryJake's heart was tender toward him, as it was toward Miz Bennett, Miss Celestine, and Hannah and her grandma. She had felt their love and their hope for her.

But she couldn't see her way ahead. She lay awake thinking over all that had been said tonight, putting it together with what Poe said in the graveyard. Before long she realized it was not Poe who was wrong because he insisted she was his sister; she was wrong because she would not accept the obvious truth. She had to be the one to set aside her angry feelings and hurt pride and accept this change in her life with a good heart.

Now as the words echoed in her memory, *There're certain tasks in life a person has to do. Hard tasks. There's no other way . . .* , she realized Ma wasn't talking only about the things MaryJake had to do. Ma was referring to herself having to admit failure by sending MaryJake back to the Kirkbanks. She was referring to herself having to give up the heirloom ring, her only security and her last tie with home. It was painful for MaryJake to let go of her belief that she was the one wronged, the only one hurt. When she did, she could even recognize that Pa might not have wanted to do some of the things he did. She finally fell asleep remembering Poe's words: "You'll win out." For the first time, she believed she would.

THIRTY-SIX

U NCLE GEORGE TOOK HANNAH to town and bought her a complete new outfit for school. He and Hannah also bought MaryJake a pair of shoes, fitted to an outline of her feet, which she had drawn on a piece of paper. The shoes were a gift of thanks to MaryJake for helping Hannah pay the dentist. Proud Hannah delivered the shoes and MaryJake accepted them for love of her friend.

MaryJake wore her new shoes and the green dress with the white leaves floating down the front the night she went with Poe to the rock castle to meet the Agnews. Miss Celestine had blunt cut MaryJake's bangs and combed her straight hair, no longer cotton white but turning true blond, so that it curled under her ears. She looked like a real girl and Poe was so pleased he could not keep from smiling the whole time.

They sat in the cool dark beneath the tree that sheltered the chairs and the swing and worked on mending their kinships. For Adelia's sake, MaryJake was careful not to let on how poor they had been or how hard they had lived. She answered their questions politely and acted mannerly as Adelia had taught her. Now she really was out in the world, as Adelia had said she would be, and she felt grateful to her for her teaching.

Erleen sat in the swing, gently swaying, and Titus sat beside Mr. Agnew on a bench, with Myra in a chair on one side of MaryJake and Poe on the other. A family circle, MaryJake thought, wondering if she could ever feel as if she belonged. From their comments MaryJake could tell that the loss of Adelia had grieved them. They asked questions about her and recalled stories about her when she was younger. They wanted MaryJake to know Adelia as she was before she left home, they explained. MaryJake felt that she herself was not yet a real person to the Agnews. They maintained a careful, friendly distance, but so did MaryJake. Adelia was their one living bond, because she was loved by all of them. And it was Adelia they talked about.

Afterward when Poe walked with her to Miz Bennett's, he explained, "You have to get to know each other. You've been so long apart, you're strangers. But it's odd—you've never been a stranger to me. Not even that first night in my yard when you thought I stole Culver." He laughed. "I feared you'd tear my house down if I didn't get him back for you."

MaryJake laughed too. "I never believed you were the varmint, no matter what Hannah's Uncle George said. Too much about you didn't fit a thief." In the silence that fell between them, MaryJake gathered her courage and said in a rush, "Are you an albino? Are you moon-eyed? Will you die?"

He stopped in the path, faced her and took both her hands. "No, my ailment is rarer than albinism. Not much is known about it, but it's inherited. You didn't inherit it, but you can pass it on to your children."

"Wha—what is it? Will it kill you like Hannah said?" MaryJake realized she was saying everything wrong, but she couldn't wait any longer to know.

"Yes, it can kill me if I'm not very careful. The least bit of sunlight does harm to me, even inside a house. To survive, I've had to reverse my life. That's why when I was fourteen, I moved down on the creek, because I didn't want the rest of the family to suffer from my way of life. I have absolutely no leeway—if I want to stay well, I live in the dark."

"Can't you be cured?"

"Our parents took me to every doctor and every clinic they could find out about that might help me—they had to wrap me in thick quilts, every inch of me—but nothing could be done. It was while we were at a hospital in Maryland that our father died—he had a massive heart attack, brought on, I'm sure, from worry over me and guilt that I had inherited the disease. I never held it against our parents. How could they help it? But I've always been glad that you don't have it."

MaryJake stood silent, thinking over all he had said.

"My ailment is not easy to say or remember," Poe continued, dropping her hands. "It's called xeroderma pigmentosum. Someday . . . someday . . . there might be something to be done for it. But for now, I don't intend to be hindered by it."

"Are you rich?" she whispered.

"I will be when I'm twenty-one. So will you. Our parents' land became mine when they died, but their money is in a trust for you and me."

MaryJake shook her head. "I don't want to be rich. I want things to stay the way they are."

Poe laughed. "Your twenty-first birthday is a while off. I don't think you need to worry about being rich just yet."

After that first family get-together, MaryJake walked to the rock castle alone on some afternoons. Erleen showed her the concealed stairway that led to the top of the tower and they climbed it to view the countryside—the stumps and washed out gullies of the deforested land and, in the distance, Poe's flourishing green forest.

Erleen played the piano with MaryJake seated beside her on the bench. MaryJake felt a thrill when Erleen selected a book of ballads and played all of the ones Adelia used to sing. MaryJake easily imagined Adelia on this same bench, playing this same music out of the old book. Titus taught MaryJake to play Chinese checkers and the two girls teamed up against Titus and Mr. Agnew.

She found out that the four of them—MaryJake, Hannah, Erleen, and Titus—would be in the same class at the school where Myra taught. School would be late opening because there was no money to pay teachers yet. MaryJake resolved to make up for lost time. She would study hard and learn everything she could about what could be done to help Hannah's grandma and Poe. Instead of a wild plant expert, perhaps she would choose to be a doctor. Why not do both? Her heart beat faster as she considered the possibility.

Nobody referred to Jake Smith or his fight with Titus.

MaryJake thought that sometime in the future when everyone knew each other better, this subject could be dealt with. MaryJake shied away from asking about Caroline Kirkbank Blanton and her husband, Robert. Poe had not forced her to hear about them. "Not until you're ready," he had said. "But I will tell you they were the finest—both of them. Combine every good trait in Myra and Adelia and you will have our mother, Caroline. And our father—he made the most ordinary kind of thing an adventure. And I sure did love him . . . and so did Caroline . . . and so did my little sister."

The most fun and laughter happened when MaryJake brought Paul and David and Hannah with her to visit. After ballgames and wild chases and exploring the rock castle, all of them crossed the road to the store for ice cream cones. Gradually they got to know Titus's friends who hung around in the shade of the store porch. MaryJake was amazed at how much she enjoyed being part of a group, which was so different from the alone kind of life she had lived before.

One night MaryJake met Poe at the graveyard to do their last job there—the raising upright of the tombstone, which they had sat on so often, and the cementing of it in its rightful place. While they worked, Poe told her that Myra and Mr. Agnew had arranged for him to assume ownership of the wasted acreage from the Kirkbank Timber Company.

"It belonged to a distant cousin who considered it worthless," he explained. "He was glad to be rid of it. The agriculture teacher at the school and his students are going to help me reforest the land. It'll be a long-term learning project for them. Besides the trees, we'll plant several acres of chufas in the spring to help bring back the wildlife. Turkeys, deer, raccoons—all of them relish chufas."

MaryJake smiled, thinking of two girls and a pig who also had an appetite for chufas. "Your dream come true," MaryJake said, "and Hannah and I will help with the chufa farming."

"Thanks, we'll need you. And thanks for offering Miss Celestine the ring to help me buy the land. Now you can keep it. I believe Adelia will come back home someday. Then it'll be here for her."

His words were so confident MaryJake felt a surge of hope. "If I could only see her again. . . . If I could only hear from her own lips why . . ." Then she whispered, "Poe Blanton, you may yet be the redemption of Jake Smith."

Afterward, they stood surveying the transformed grave-yard in the light from a lantern hanging on the gate. They complimented each other on a hard job well done.

Neither of them noticed how clouds had covered the stars until large raindrops began splattering them. They hurried to store their tools and gloves in the shed and ran through the rain to Miz Bennett's.

Miss Celestine stirred from her pallet on the porch, wrapped Barbrie Allen's Rose around herself, and sat with them, watching the lightning dance among the treetops. Between the thunder noise she said, "Tomorrow Dink and I take up our search again. This has been our longest rest ever, but the Lord knew we needed it. He spoke to me with that celestial show. I regret I've been slow to obey Him. I've put my own desires first. But now we're going."

"In six months or so, we'll expect you again," Poe said.

"We'll have the lean-to built by then, maybe two of them. You won't have to sleep on the porch."

"If you come across Ma and Pa," MaryJake said steadily, "tell them where we are."

Miss Celestine agreed she would, and they sat in silence while the storm thrashed round about the little house. MaryJake was unafraid, content to be where she was, smelling the freshness of the rain slanting down in the dark, rain that looked as shining silver as her brother Poe.

AFTERWORD

THE PERIOD OF "hard times" in which MaryJake lived was called by many names—"one of America's bleakest periods," "the worst economic debacle in Western memory," "the maelstrom," "an unprecedented calamity," "an economic cataclysm," "a dismal tragedy." Even if you didn't know the meaning of some of those words, the very sound of them is chilling. The most commonly used term, however, is the Great Depression. The United States had experienced depressions before, but never one so devastating as that of the 1930s.

Alabama, the state where MaryJake lived and where I grew up, suffered severely during this era. Most Alabamians depended on farming for a living, but prices for the harvest fell to an all-time low. New crops could not grow because of drought, floods, hail storms, boll weevils, and other insect pests. Erosion had washed deep gullies in the fields and carried away topsoil. Thousands of families lost their farms because of debt.

Those who took refuge in cities found few jobs available, even for skilled workmen. Birmingham, the city nearest MaryJake, was the hardest-hit city in the entire country, according to the president of the United States, Franklin Roosevelt. Hordes of homeless wanderers lived in parks, under viaducts, in vacant houses, and in "hobo jungles" near the railroad tracks. Crowds of the hungry foraged, and sometimes fought over, the garbage they found behind restaurants and in alleys. Those fortunate few with some kind of motorized vehicle loaded it with their children and possessions and headed west with hope in their desperate hearts, as MaryJake's ma and pa did. Thousands of others, young and old, traveled the country in all directions, "thumbing" rides on the highway or hopping freight trains. Detectives, hired by the railroads to remove illegal riders, evicted as many as a thousand in one night on the short run from Birmingham to Montgomery.

Sometimes parents who were unable to feed and clothe their children gave a child away, perhaps to a relative or to a better-off neighbor. Christopher Paul Curtis, in his Newbery Medal winner *Bud, Not Buddy,* a book that takes place during the Great Depression, points out in his afterword that the suffering from 1929 to 1941 was so terrible that "countless thousands" of children were abandoned by their parents.

Most people had no way to go places except on foot. If someone became ill, families depended on home remedies because they had no way to carry the patient to a doctor and no money to pay the bill. Two of my classmates died during the 1930s for lack of medical care, one from tetanus and the other from appendicitis.

Some of these tragic conditions I heard about, others I saw as I grew up on a farm at Brookwood, Alabama. Blood-red sunrises and sunsets covered nearly the whole sky, as a result of the dust blown from the ruined farms of the Midwest. As I hoed cotton, I watched hitchhikers walking along the road going somewhere, anywhere. Hardly a day went by without one or more of these wanderers knocking on our back door to ask for food or shelter. One cold night my mother took in a very old man who was walking westward with his small granddaughter. She not only fed them supper and breakfast but also put clean sheets on the best bed in our house for their night's rest.

We were forced to use what we had to make what we needed. My mother saved grease from cooking, mixed it with lye, and boiled it into soap in a black iron wash pot in our backyard. She bleached fertilizer sacks, dyed them a rich brown using walnut hulls, and made dresses for my sisters and me. She used my grandmother's treadle sewing machine to sew for us late into the night, and she worked long hours in the hot sun taking care of her vegetable garden.

We children did chores around the house and carried water twice a day from a spring about a mile away. We roamed the countryside picking blackberries, which my mother turned into cobblers and jelly. We knew where the plum thickets were and brought home buckets of ripe plums for eating and for jam making.

My father was one of the millions of men without a job. Searching for work, he walked eastward to Birmingham, westward to Tuscaloosa—hungry, cold, and despairing in winter, hungry, hot, and hopeless in summer. Uppermost on his mind were his wife and five children at home with endless needs: food, shelter, clothing, schoolbooks, medical and dental care. In similar circumstances, many men deserted their families, but my father stayed faithful to us. I remember how thin and careworn he looked. He finally got work on the "extra" board of a railroad, which meant he could be called at any time to go to work anywhere in several states. Some months he wasn't called at all; other months he might be called away from home for three or four weeks at a time.

There were few opportunities for young people to earn money. My sister and her friend dug sassafras roots and sold them to townspeople for making tea. They also rode trained calves along the highway, as MaryJake and Hannah did, collecting bottles to sell to the local moonshiner. Poor as Hannah's family was, they could afford to let her have two calves for riding (and ploughing when needed) because calves were cheap to support. They required one-tenth of the food a mule needed, yet they could work as hard as a mule.

School systems in the thirties lacked money to pay the teachers and heat the buildings. My school opened late, as did MaryJake's and Hannah's, and in 1932 the term ended before Christmas. No one in MaryJake's settlement had a telephone. When I was growing up, the nearest telephone was in a store two miles away. I knew only one person who owned a radio. I remember standing in her yard, listening through the open window to President Roosevelt giving his famous speech in which he told all Americans, "The only thing we have to fear is fear itself."

During the Depression, we saw many "shooting stars" but no meteorites. To describe the one that MaryJake and Hannah sold to Mr. Hollister I combined two real meteorites—one that fell in May 1879 in Estherville, Iowa, and another that fell in November 1954 at Sylacauga, Alabama. My husband's grandfather witnessed the fall of the Estherville meteorite, and for many years his family had a piece of it, which he had collected. The Sylacauga meteorite is the only one known to have struck a person, Ann Hodges, for whom it was named. At first no one realized that there was a second, smaller piece of the Sylacauga meteorite until Mr. J. K. McKinney discovered it. Or rather, his mules discovered it. They were pulling a wagon load of wood collected by Mr. McKinney along a dirt road in the forest when they suddenly stopped and refused to move. Mr. McKinney got down from the wagon, expecting to find a snake in the road. But the only thing he saw was a strange ugly rock that he threw off into the woods. Then the mules were willing to continue on their way home. When later he heard what had happened to Mrs. Hodges, Mr. McKinney returned to the woods and found the rock. It proved to be a part of the Hodges meteorite. He sold it to the Smithsonian Institution. Mrs. Hodges gave hers to the Museum of Natural History at the University of Alabama in Tuscaloosa. Parts of the Estherville meteorite can be seen at the University of Minnesota in Minneapolis, and at the Estherville Public Library in Estherville, Iowa.

Here are a few books that show the Great Depression in photographs:

Agee, James, and Walker Evans. *Let Us Now Praise Famous Men*. New York: Houghton Mifflin, 1941.

Editors of Time-Life Books. *Hard Times: The 30s.* Alexandria, Va.: Time-Life Books, 1998.

Thomason, Michael V. R. *Trying Times: Alabama Photographs, 1917–1945.* Tuscaloosa: University of Alabama Press, 1985.

ACKNOWLEDGMENTS

DURING THE DEPRESSION our government
encouraged farmers to grow chufas, or chufa nuts,
a nourishing plant that originated in Egypt. Mr. Bill
Hubbard of Vance, Alabama, recalled for me how delicious chufas were. Like MaryJake and Hannah, he and his
brothers carried around pocketsful of them to munch. Mr.
Wayne Ford, a county agent from Tuscaloosa, Alabama,
furnished me with historical information about chufas.

I give ardent thanks to Henrietta Mims, who is a
librarian at the Birmingham Veterans Hospital, and to
Cynthia Cockerham, a librarian at the Lister Hill Library
of the Health Sciences at the University of Alabama,
Birmingham, for their research of xeroderma pigmentosum, the rare disorder affecting Poe.

I owe a heartfelt thank you to Dr. Eason K. Wood, a
dentist in Tuscaloosa, Alabama, who helped me understand what had to be done to Hannah's teeth.

Thanks also to Dr. John Hall of the University of
Alabama Museum of Natural History for providing me

with information on the Sylacauga meteorite, and to Dr. Calvin Alexander of the University of Minnesota for information on the Estherville meteorite.

And to Emilie Buchwald, my editor: I am most grateful for her painstaking critique of the manuscript that eventually became *Hard Times for Jake Smith*.

AILEEN KILGORE HENDERSON grew up in Alabama, where she resides in Brookwood. She served in the Women's Army Corps during World War II as an airplane engine mechanic and a photo lab technician. After the war she graduated from the University of Alabama and taught school in Northport, Alabama; Big Bend National Park, Texas; and Stillwater, Minnesota. She has worked with children and adults as a docent in historical museums, art museums, and a home for abused women and children. Her first book for children, *The Summer of the Bonepile Monster*, won the Milkweed Prize for Children's Literature and the Alabama Library Association Award. Her second book for children, *The Monkey Thief*, was selected for the New York Public Library's list of *1998 Books for the Teen Age*. She is also the author of *The Treasure of Panther Peak*, which was placed on the Sunshine State Young Reader's list.

IF YOU ENJOYED THIS BOOK,
YOU'LL ALSO WANT TO READ THESE OTHER
MILKWEED NOVELS.

To order books or for more information, contact Milkweed at
(800) 520-6455 or visit our website (www.milkweed.org).

The $66 Summer
by John Armistead

MILKWEED PRIZE FOR CHILDREN'S LITERATURE
NEW YORK PUBLIC LIBRARY BEST BOOKS OF THE YEAR:
"BOOKS FOR THE TEEN AGE"

By working at his grandmother's general store in Obadiah, Alabama, during the summer of 1955, George Harrington figures he can save enough money to buy the motorcycle he wants, a Harley-Davidson. Spending his off-hours with two friends, Esther Garrison, fourteen, and Esther's younger brother, Bennett, the unusual trio in 1950s Alabama—George is white and Esther and Bennett are black—embark on a summer of adventure that turns serious when they begin to uncover the truth about the racism in their midst.

The Return of Gabriel
by John Armistead

When Cooper Grant, Jubal Harris, and Squirrel Kogan form a secret society called the Scorpions, they set their sights on getting even with the school bully, Reno McCarthy. But it's 1964, and as civil rights workers descend on their small Mississippi town and the KKK gathers to respond, tension begins to rise. The boys' camaraderie and courage are tested as each is swept up into the tumultuous events of "Freedom Summer."

Gildaen, The Heroic Adventures of a Most Unusual Rabbit
by Emilie Buchwald

CHICAGO TRIBUNE BOOK FESTIVAL AWARD, BEST BOOK FOR AGES 9—12

Gildaen is befriended by a mysterious being who has lost his memory but not the ability to change shape at will. Together they accept the perilous task of thwarting the evil sorcerer, Grimald, in this tale of magic, villainy, and heroism.

The Ocean Within
by V. M. Caldwell

MILKWEED PRIZE FOR CHILDREN'S LITERATURE

Elizabeth is a foster child who has just been placed with the boisterous and affectionate Sheridans, a family that wants to adopt her. Accustomed to having to fend for herself, however, Elizabeth is reluctant to open up to them. During a summer spent by the ocean with the eight Sheridan children and their grandmother, dubbed by Elizabeth as "Iron Woman" because of her strict discipline, Elizabeth learns what it means—and how much she must risk—to become a permanent member of a loving family.

Tides
by V. M. Caldwell

Recently adopted twelve-year-old Elizabeth Sheridan is looking forward to spending the summer at Grandma's oceanside home. But during her stay there, she faces problems involving her cousins, five-year-old Petey and eighteen-year-old Adam, that cause her to question whether the family will hold together. As she and Grandma help each other through troubling times, Elizabeth comes to see that she has become an important member of the family.

Alligator Crossing
by Marjory Stoneman Douglas

Near the strange wilderness that forms Everglades National Park, young Henry Bunks has made a secret hideaway for himself to which he can flee from the teasing and bullying of his older schoolmates. In this tense and colorful story, the hideaway becomes the starting place for a string of adventures involving an outlaw alligator hunter, a roving botanist, a girl traveling with her father in a palatial cruiser, and, above all, the vast Everglades. Setting and story are tautly linked as Henry finds himself serving the alligator hunter first as unwilling accomplice and finally as rescuer.

Parents Wanted
by George Harrar

MILKWEED PRIZE FOR CHILDREN'S LITERATURE

After five "adoption parties" and no luck, Andy Fleck, the kid nobody wanted, faces his biggest challenge yet—learning how to live with parents who seem to love him. Placed in an adoptive home with Jeff and Laurie, he has a chance to get out of the grip of his past, which includes a jailed father and a mother who gave him up to the state. But Andy can't keep himself from challenging every limit that his adoptive parents set. So far, Laurie and Jeff have refused to give up on their difficult new son. But will he go too far?

The Trouble with Jeremy Chance
by George Harrar

The year is 1919 and Jeremy Chance is stuck at home in Derry, New Hampshire, while his brother Davey is fighting overseas. When Jeremy and his father have a disagreement, and Jeremy is unfairly punished for it, he decides to run away to Boston to meet his returning brother. But Jeremy has no way of knowing that the morning he sets foot in Boston will be the day of the great molasses explosion. By the end of the day, Jeremy will be an unlikely hero, and he will also find a way to forgive his father.

No Place
by Kay Haugaard

Arturo Morales and his fellow sixth-grade classmates decide to improve their neighborhood and their lives by building a park in their otherwise concrete, inner-city Los Angeles barrio. The kids are challenged by their teachers to figure out what it would take to transform the neighborhood junkyard into a clean, safe place for children to play. Despite their parents' skepticism and the threat of street gangs, Arturo and his classmates struggle to prove that the actions of individuals—even kids—can make a difference.

The Monkey Thief
by Aileen Kilgore Henderson

NEW YORK PUBLIC LIBRARY BEST BOOKS OF THE YEAR:
"BOOKS FOR THE TEEN AGE"

Twelve-year-old Steve Hanson is sent to Costa Rica for eight months to live with his uncle. There he discovers a world completely unlike anything he can see from the cushions of his couch back home, a world filled with giant trees and insects, mysterious sounds, and the constant companionship of monkeys swinging in the branches overhead. When Steve hatches a plan to capture a monkey for himself, his quest for a pet leads him into dangerous territory. It takes all of Steve's survival skills—and the help of his new friends—to get him out of trouble.

The Summer of the Bonepile Monster
by Aileen Kilgore Henderson

MILKWEED PRIZE FOR CHILDREN'S LITERATURE
ALABAMA LIBRARY ASSOCIATION 1996 JUVENILE/YOUNG ADULT AWARD
MAUDE HART LOVELACE AWARD FINALIST

Eleven-year-old Hollis Orr has been sent to spend the summer with Grancy, his father's grandmother, in rural Dolliver, Alabama, while his parents "work things out." As summer begins, Hollis encounters a road called Bonepile Hollow, barred by a gate and a real skull and crossbones mounted on a board. "Things that go down that road don't ever come back," he is told. Thus begins the mystery that plunges Hollis into real danger.

Treasure of Panther Peak
by Aileen Kilgore Henderson
NEW YORK PUBLIC LIBRARY BEST BOOKS OF THE YEAR: "BOOKS FOR THE TEEN AGE"

Twelve-year-old Page Williams begrudgingly accompanies her mother, Ellie, as she flees her abusive husband, Page's father. Together they settle in a fantastic new world—Big Bend National Park, Texas. Wild animals stalk through the park, and the nearby Ghost Mountains are filled with legends of lost treasures. As Page tests her limits by sneaking into forbidden canyons, Ellie struggles to win the trust of other parents. Only through their newfound courage are they able to discover a treasure beyond what they could have imagined.

I Am Lavina Cumming
by Susan Lowell
MOUNTAINS & PLAINS BOOKSELLERS ASSOCIATION AWARD

In 1905, ten-year-old Lavina is sent from her home on the Bosque Ranch in Arizona Territory to live with her aunt in the city of Santa Cruz, California. Armed with the Cumming family motto, "courage," Lavina deals with a new school, homesickness, a very spoiled cousin, an earthquake, and a big decision about her future.

The Boy with Paper Wings
by Susan Lowell

Confined to bed with a viral fever, eleven-year-old Paul sails a paper airplane into his closet and propels himself into mysterious and dangerous realms in this exciting and fantastical adventure. Paul finds himself trapped in the military diorama on his closet floor, out to stop the evil commander, KRON. Armed only with paper and the knowledge of how to fold it, Paul uses his imagination and courage to find his way out of dilemmas and disasters.

The Secret of the Ruby Ring
by Yvonne MacGrory

WINNER OF IRELAND'S BISTO "BOOK OF THE YEAR" AWARD

Lucy gets a very special birthday present, a star ruby ring, from her grandmother and finds herself transported to Langley Castle in the Ireland of 1885. At first, she is intrigued by castle life, in which she is the lowliest servant, until she loses the ruby ring and her only way home.

Emma and the Ruby Ring
by Yvonne MacGrory

Only one day short of her eleventh birthday and looking forward to spending time with her dad, Emma wakes up not at her cousin Lucy's, where she has been visiting, but in a nineteenth-century Irish workhouse. Emma learns that the ruby ring can grant two wishes to its wearer, and now, at a time of dire historical unrest, she must prove she can be the heroic girl she wants to be.

A Bride for Anna's Papa
by Isabel R. Marvin

Life on Minnesota's iron range in 1907 is not easy for thirteen-year-old Anna Kallio. Her mother's death has left Anna to take care of the house, her young brother, and her father, a blacksmith in the dangerous iron mines. So she and her brother plot to find their father a new wife, even attempting to arrange a match with one of the "mail order" brides arriving from Finland.

Minnie
by Annie M. G. Schmidt

Miss Minnie is a cat. Or rather, she *was* a cat. She is now a human, and she's not at all happy to be one. As Minnie tries to find and reverse the cause of her transformation, she brings her reporter friend, Mr. Tibbs, news from the cats' gossip hotline—including revealing information that one of the town's most prominent citizens is not the animal lover he appears to be.

The Dog with Golden Eyes
by Frances Wilbur

Many girls dream of owning a dog of their own, but Cassie's wish for one takes an unexpected turn in this contemporary tale of friendship and growing up. Thirteen-year-old Cassie is lonely, bored, and feeling friendless when a large, beautiful dog appears one day in her suburban backyard. Cassie wants to adopt the dog, but as she learns more about him, she realizes that she is, in fact, caring for a full-grown Arctic wolf. As she attempts to protect the wolf from urban dangers, Cassie discovers that she possesses strengths and resources she never imagined.

Behind the Bedroom Wall
by Laura E. Williams

MILKWEED PRIZE FOR CHILDREN'S LITERATURE
NEW YORK PUBLIC LIBRARY BEST BOOKS OF THE YEAR:
"BOOKS FOR THE TEEN AGE"
MAUDE HART LOVELACE AWARD FINALIST
SUNSHINE STATE YOUNG READER'S AWARD MASTER LIST
JANE ADDAMS PEACE AWARD HONOR BOOK

It is 1942. Thirteen-year-old Korinna Rehme is an active member of her local *Jungmädel*, a Nazi youth group, along with many of her friends. Korinna's parents, however, secretly are members of an underground group providing a means of escape to the Jews of their city and are, in fact, hiding a refugee family behind the wall of Korinna's bedroom. As Korinna comes to know the family, especially their young daughter, her sympathies begin to turn. But when someone tips off the Gestapo, loyalties are put to the test and Korinna must decide in what she believes and whom she trusts.

The Spider's Web
by Laura E. Williams

Thirteen-year-old Lexi Jordan has just joined the Pack, a group of neo-Nazi skinheads, as a substitute for the close-knit family she wishes she had. After she and the Pack spray paint a synagogue, Lexi hides from her pursuers on the front porch of elderly Ursula

Zeidler's home, a former member of the Hitler Youth Group, who painfully recalls her ugly anti-Semitic Nazi activities and betrayal of a friend. When her younger sister becomes enthralled with Lexi's new "family," Lexi realizes the true meaning of the Pack and has little time to save herself and her sister from its sinister grip.

MILKWEED EDITIONS publishes with the intention of making a humane impact on society, in the belief that literature is a transformative art uniquely able to convey the essential experiences of the human heart and spirit. To that end, Milkweed publishes distinctive voices of literary merit in handsomely designed, visually dynamic books, exploring the ethical, cultural, and esthetic issues that free societies need continually to address. Milkweed Editions is a not-for-profit press.

JOIN US

Since its genesis as *Milkweed Chronicle* in 1979, Milkweed has helped hundreds of emerging writers reach their readers. Thanks to the generosity of foundations and of individuals like you, Milkweed Editions is able to continue its nonprofit mission of publishing books chosen on the basis of literary merit—of how they impact the human heart and spirit—rather than on how they impact the bottom line. That's a miracle our readers have made possible.

In addition to purchasing Milkweed books, you can join the growing community of Milkweed supporters. Individual contributions of any amount are both meaningful and welcome. Contact us for a Milkweed catalog or log on to www.milkweed.org and click on "About Milkweed," then "Supporting Milkweed," to find out about our donor program, or simply call (800) 520-6455 and ask about becoming one of Milkweed's contributors. As a nonprofit press, Milkweed belongs to you, the community. Milkweed's board, its staff, and especially the authors whose careers you help launch thank you for reading our books and supporting our mission in any way you can.

Interior design by Christian Fünfhausen.
Typeset in 11/15 point Goudy Old Style BT Roman
by Stanton Publication Services.
Printed on acid-free 55# New Leaf Eco Book
100 recycled paper
by Friesen Corporation.